Crusade

By the same author

The Night of the Burning

Crusade

LINDA PRESS WULF

BLOOMSBURY

LONDON BERLIN NEW YORK SYDNEY

Bloomsbury Publishing, London, Berlin, New York and Sydney

First published in Great Britain in January 2011 by Bloomsbury Publishing Plc
36 Soho Square, London, W1D 3QY

A CIP catalogue record of this book is available from the British Library

ISBN 978 1 4088 0484 1

Typeset by Hewer Text UK Ltd, Edinburgh
Printed in Great Britain by Clays Ltd, St Ives Plc, Bungay, Suffolk

1 3 5 7 9 10 8 6 4 2

www.bloomsbury.com

To my husband, Stanley, my stalwart companion on the long and rewarding journey
To my brother, Don, who inspired me to love history and helped to shape this book

FRANCE, 1212

PART ONE

The Children's Crusade

CHAPTER ONE

Foundling. Orphan. Parish child. All these names belonged to him but he didn't want to belong to them.

Robert le Corde, Robert the Rope, he was also called by the children in his neighbourhood, because of the knobbly scar, red and raised, that stretched like an unevenly coiled rope all the way from the outside of his eyebrow down to below his ear, at the jaw line. He had been trying to evade a crowd of such tormentors when he had scrambled up an ironwork gate and fallen, gouging the side of his head on the sharp iron points protruding from the top.

The barber-surgeon had shrugged his shoulders helplessly when he was called to tend to the unconscious little boy. The deep cut began too close to the eye for the barber to try sewing it together and all he could do was to give his most sagacious opinion: the boy would survive the injury if he didn't die.

Robert had been carried into the nearby church, the only church situated among the higgledy-piggledy huts in this poor neighbourhood on the outskirts of the city of Tours. The city's residents came here to dump their rubbish into the Loire. Children scavenged in the refuse on the riverbanks for anything that could be eaten or sold. Robert had slept on the floor of the church since he was a toddler, always at a little distance from the others who had no home.

After Robert's accident, a kind priest had covered him with a blanket and brought him a bowl of gruel once a day. That was the extent of his nursing. There had been no wise woman to dress the wound with the whites of newly broken eggs or spread aromatic balsam to seal the hideous gash, no mother to massage the newly formed scar every day to press it flat. Whether he lived or died had been in the hands of the Lord. Whether there was minor or major scarring had been in those hands too.

Robert lived, but with a highly visible reminder of the accident. He flushed and averted his face whenever he was teased. Soon after the local children coined his new name, he took to wearing a loose, black hood over his head at all times, slipping it off only in the dimness of the church. He slept in front of the fire in the church kitchen and ate whatever food he was given in charity by the priests. He was often hungry but he never stole food like the other orphans in the town. This was not the result of adult influence or supervision. He had been born with an inviolable sense of right and wrong.

He also appeared to have been born with unusual intelligence. Hearing matins and vespers every day as he did, he was able to chant the liturgy by the time he was six years old, an accomplishment that was to change his life a year later.

One evening, the abbot of the large Abbey of Blois made an unscheduled stop just outside the church. An axle on his carriage had broken just as he was leaving Tours to return to the abbey across the river, and he was forced to take shelter for the night until the blacksmith could mend the axle in the light of day. It would be undignified for him to walk back to his hosts in the centre of Tours, and so he accepted the offer of a night's accommodation in the church.

For a man with the abbot's drive and ambition, this sudden waste of a night's work was very trying. However, his iron self-control did not permit him to show his irritation.

He was invited to lead the priests at vespers.

'Thank you, but I have a slight headache,' the abbot replied. 'I will be glad to pray quietly in a pew on my own.'

The truth was that the abbot intended to use the inconvenient delay to muse over some sensitive church business. Motionless in a dark corner, he was almost forgotten as vespers was chanted. A painter would not have been inspired by his stern face and rigid posture. But if a surgeon could have delicately sliced open the abbot's scalp and revealed the man's musings, he would have marvelled at the crystal precision of the abbot's thoughts and the subtle shading of his calculations.

Viewers would look in vain, however, for the deep red pulse of emotion, or even the soft pink tissue of sentimentality. The abbot was not touched by the sight of a scar-faced little boy helping the priest at vespers, wearing a discarded habit so big for him that he had to lift the trailing skirt to walk. But his curiosity was aroused by the evident fluency of the lad's Latin as he recited the liturgy of the hour. Only a few candles wavered in the deep gloom of the church, so the boy could not have been watching the lips of the priest: he had to have learned the lengthy service by heart.

'Who has been teaching that child?' he asked of the priest who was his host for the night.

'Ah, you mean little Robert,' the man said. 'No one has to teach him. He has a memory more remarkable than any other I have encountered. He breathes in knowledge like air. He is a bastard, you know, a foundling left at the door of the church when he was but three years old, but I suspect that his father, or even perhaps his mother, did not come from the ranks of our illiterate congregation.'

The abbot asked no more questions, but after matins and lauds the next morning he called the little boy to him. The boy looked up timidly at the imposing figure in a severe black cloak.

'I heard you chant vespers yesterday, and today you said matins and lauds alongside the priest, boy,' the abbot observed without any preliminaries. 'Can you recite them on your own?'

The boy did not reply directly but began to chant the Latin, perfectly, without hesitating over a single word.

'What is thirteen plus seven minus three, boy?'

The boy's face was blank. Clearly he had never learned the concepts of addition or subtraction. But when the abbot told him a complicated story of some boys playing with pebbles in the street, exchanging this one for two of those and losing certain numbers of their stones along the way, the boy listened with interest and then told the abbot exactly how many pebbles were in the pocket of each boy when they ended their playing for the day.

The abbot observed him silently for a minute, and then drew three letters on a dusty tombstone with his long finger.

'Can you tell me the names and sounds of those letters, boy?' he enquired.

'No, Père Abbé, I cannot read yet. But I hope to find someone who will teach me one day,' Robert answered eagerly.

'This is a "b", this an "a", and the last one is a "d",' the abbot told him. 'The first one takes the sound *b-b-b*, the second one makes the sound *a-a-a*, and the last one sounds like *d-d-d*.'

Robert's dark eyes were focused intently on the streaks in the dust.

'If you want to read what they say together, you make the sounds aloud. *B . . . a . . . d . . . B-a-d. Bad.* So the letters together say *bad*. Do you understand?'

Robert nodded vigorously.

'Now, I will write a different word,' said the abbot, printing *Dab* below the other. 'You have to remember the sounds of each letter in the previous word. Then you will be able to read this word too.'

Robert examined the scribbling on the ground. He murmured to himself for a while, and then raised his eyes.

'*D-a-b*. It says *dab*. Is that correct, Père Abbé?'

The abbot smiled thinly. 'It is correct.' Then he dismissed Robert, and he went to talk to the priest who had told him about the boy.

The mended carriage left the church courtyard that morning carrying a little extra weight. It was the boy's first journey out of Tours and across the river. He was unnerved by the frigid manner of his august new guardian, Abbot Benedict, but also overwhelmed with joy at his sudden and unexpected good fortune. He was to live in a rich monastery called Blois. He was to eat three times a day – after waiting on Abbot Benedict's needs first, of course. Most incredibly, he was to be taught to read and write so that he could help the abbot with his heavy burden of work. He was going to be educated to make him a credit to the abbot. He shivered with excitement and then gave a happy bounce on the springy seat.

'Stop fidgeting, Robert,' Abbot Benedict ordered. 'Clasp your hands on your lap as I do, look straight ahead of you and keep still.'

Robert obeyed immediately. For this extraordinary chance, he would have jumped down to the road and run all the way alongside the unsmiling man in his black carriage. Certainly he could keep quiet and stay still, for years, if required.

CHAPTER TWO

Gregor glared into his steaming pottage, and Georgette stepped carefully around him – it was wise not to disturb Gregor when he was in one of his moods. He could suddenly lash out like a tomcat leaping from a tree branch, grab Georgette's white-blonde plaits and yank them with all his might, making her shriek with pain. Or he might kick her shins with the tip of the broken old leather boots he'd found at the side of the road outside their village of Illiers.

Georgette grew up under the rough care of her father and the rougher ministrations of her brother. Her mother had died when she was born and her father had flatly refused to give her and her older brother to a childless couple who wanted them as their own. It was not clear whether this unusual choice was due to stubborn pride or fierce love. But it was indisputable that he was only seventeen years old at the time and had neither experience nor aptitude as a nurturing parent.

Once, when Georgette, then a little girl, went crying to her father about Gregor's wild temper, her father said that the Devil had got into Gregor when his mother died. Georgette's forehead wrinkled. What could their mother's death have to do with the Devil entering Gregor? What was the Devil doing inside Gregor? And why didn't someone get it out? But her father was a man of few words and he had used up all those he was going to employ that day. She was left to ponder the problem alone.

Gregor's rages were bad enough when he was unprovoked, but they rose to a fever pitch when the other boys of the village taunted him. They plotted ways to awaken his anger from a safe distance, and then laughed at his hoarse roars and wild charges. Only his father and sister used his given name. Adults and children of the village alike called him *Soupe au lait*, because soup with milk in it comes to a boil so quickly. Georgette learned that the only times she was quite safe were those days when Gregor crawled home injured and spent. That meant he had been in a fight that day and had managed to satisfy his rage in the brawl.

One would have expected the toddler to latch on to the first gentle female available to nurture her. But she turned to yet another male, albeit one in skirts: the old priest who lived in a simple hut behind the village church, Father David.

No one remembered when the strange attachment began, but Georgette learned to walk by holding on to the skirt of the priest's worn habit, learned to talk by babbling the soft murmuring she heard as he recited endless *Ave*s and *Noster*s, and puzzled her little friend Patrice at the village pond by forsaking the making of mud pies to scratch tiny shapes in the sand instead.

'What are you making, Georgette? Why are you holding the stick that way?'

No woman had ever sung a lullaby to Georgette, but she was soothed by the priest's gentle voice as he led the way through the psalter, accompanied by the only two boys whose fathers were wealthy enough to pay the priest to tutor them. As she played, she lisped the alphabet like a comforting incantation, as another child her age would sing a nursery rhyme. She could be quiet too, amusing herself for hours by copying again and again with her fingertip the spidery letters the priest had carved at her request on a piece of white birch bark. Neither she nor Father David was surprised when she wrote her first words, but by mutual and silent agreement neither of them ever mentioned to Georgette's father or brother, or to anyone else in the village, almost all of them illiterate, that she could read and write by the time she was seven.

She learned other skills too. From the village woman who helped care for the priest for a few hours each day, she learned to boil the buttermilk he enjoyed, straining out the solids before pouring it into his mug. She learned to fry eggs with honey so that he could swallow them more easily, and to bake apples until they were soft, sprinkling them with very finely chopped nuts. She learned to cook more hearty fare too and soon took over the cooking in her own home. She watched carefully and learned to spin, weave and sew while Patrice and the other little girls were out playing.

When she turned nine, the woman who had cooked and cleaned for Father David fell ill and died. From then on, the priest solemnly and regularly paid Georgette a coin – which she immediately gave to her father – for making his simple meals, scrubbing the trestle table where he taught and read and wrote, and carefully dusting the concertina folds of parchment in the leather-bound codices that were all the wealth he had retained when he renounced his privileged life.

Father David was very particular about penmanship. As he copied a manuscript, he justified the physical pleasure he took in the flowing ink, as shiny as a raven's wing, and the curving letters, sinuous and showy, by quoting Saint Bernard: 'Every word you write is a blow that smites the Devil.' Georgette nodded her head vigorously as she practised her own letters.

What Georgette's father thought of the close relationship between his daughter and the most respected man in the village, he never said. He was heard to boast once, when he had drunk too much beer at the festival after the harvest, that his daughter was learning alongside the priest's two rich pupils. But the incredulous guffaws of his drinking companions sobered him, and he shut his mouth.

The villagers held the priest in high esteem, not for his excellent education as the scholarly youngest son of a noble family, but because, unlike the priests in the surrounding villages, he did not demand a tithe from them. Indeed, it was a very great relief in their hard lives not to have to hand over to the priest a tenth of everything they produced: not only a tenth of the original produce, like wheat, but of the finished food too, like flour; not only every tenth chicken, but every tenth egg too. For that and other deeds, they appreciated and loved him, and gladly brought him little gifts of food – a bowl of white cheese, a rough loaf of bread, the berry liqueur that stained their fingers a rich red.

The priest was growing frail and his eyesight was poor. But he could still see deeply into the eyes of each of the villagers at confession, and he measured out the difficulty of the penance by what he saw there. He never demanded the usual payments for absolution – a fattened duck for the priest's dinner, a load of firewood for the priest's stove. No, Father David gave penances that were strange but hard in their own way: a woman who confessed she had sold old eggs as fresh should deliver a basket of eggs anonymously at night to the poorest house in the village; or a villager who had slandered another had to provide an honest apology and a day's help in the fields. Those passing near the little church heard the thunder of his voice as he detailed for a notorious husband the excruciating pain suffered in the world to come by men who struck women or children, and to the battered family's incredulous relief the man kept his fists to himself the next few times he staggered home late from the inn.

That particular warning was not prompted by an admission of wrongdoing in the confessional, for the husband had never thought it wrong to discipline his wife, but by the priest's intimate knowledge of his flock. The same insight led him to warn the blacksmith's wife of the fate awaiting adulterers on the Day of Judgement, before she had done any more than draw out her laundry time at the village pond when a handsome young neighbour brought his horses to drink.

'How did he know I was the one who broke the church window?' Patrice demanded of Georgette. 'He was visiting sick old Dame Villeneuve when the stone that I kicked cracked his glass, and I told no one. But at confession he kept asking me what other sin weighed on my conscience, what other sin, what other sin, until I broke down and told him, and then all he said was, "Don't you feel better now, Patrice, my child?"'

This was the same gentle man who had stood little Georgette on her feet when she fell and soothed her minor injuries. And the same man who loved Jesus Christ as tenderly, intimately, dearly as a son, father, brother. Georgette's faith was watered by the tears the priest wept when he told her of the crucifixion. She cried too, and the old man and the little girl sat together, discussing with grief the Saviour's suffering in every detail, praying to God to forgive wicked mankind for the pain inflicted on His only son.

Once, Father David caught her hobbling on a stone she had inserted in her little felt shoe, and he made her take it out. He explained firmly that punishing her own body would not remove one part of the pain of our Lord and might even add to it. What father would not feel hurt at the hurt of his own child?

Georgette had heard of other priests placing small pebbles inside their shoes, causing them to hobble and bleed. Some wore rough, scratchy animal-hair shirts that chafed against the skin under their habits. Thus could one's soul be cleansed and forgiveness earned, they proclaimed. But what her priest said made sense to her and she did not mortify her flesh again.

However, she longed to do something difficult to prove her deep love for God. She sometimes cried as she dusted the sacred statues, including the painted wooden carving of perfect Mother Mary in her sky-blue gown. Father David said that Mother Mary was especially Georgette's mother because she had no mother of her own. His mother too, he told her, had died in childbirth, and the mother he had chosen to devote himself to was the Mother Church.

Georgette loved her birth father, of course, but not with passionate reverence. Her father on this earth was an impassive man who seemed much older than his young years, his face rarely showing emotion, his devotion to his children and to God unexpressed. Instead, his coin of currency was hard work. That was his declaration of love, that was his religion, although he would have thought such an avowal to be heresy.

He rose before sunrise, urinated out of the door, lit the fire, and set the porridge to cook on the hearth in the middle of their single-room hut. Then he milked the two goats and fed the horse before returning to the house to stir warm frothy goats' milk into the boiling porridge and sop it up with the hunk of bread Georgette had wrapped in a cloth and set out for him the previous night. On a cold day he might swing a sheepskin cape over the woollen smock and breeches he wore day and night without a change. He shouldered his scythe, spade and pitchfork, harnessed the horse, clicked his tongue, and strode off alongside the animal to cut the wheat field below the lower edge of the village or to sow rye in another field half a mile across the valley floor, or to break up clods in a barley field even more distant. None of the three fields belonged to him. Like the rest of the land that spread as far as the eye could see, the fields were owned by King Philippe Auguste and managed by his bailiffs. As payment for his heavy labour, he was allowed to take the crops from the smallest field for eating or selling.

Soon after their father left for the fields, Gregor rolled off his straw pallet, his mood almost always black in the mornings. He shovelled a double helping of porridge into his mouth in surly silence, washing it down with the lees of the wine from the previous night. He wrapped some dry bread, cured meat or cheese, and a flagon of cider in a piece of cloth, and tied the bundle to his shepherd's crook. Then he was off to the rich pastures up in the mountains with their two goats, as well as a dozen goats and sheep belonging to neighbours who paid him in kind to shepherd their flocks. He was an accurate shot with a bow and arrow, and most days he brought home a squirrel or hare or maybe even a pheasant for their dinner.

When it was the season to harvest the grain, Gregor joined in with the entire village as they shared these communal tasks, but he was prickly and oversensitive with the other boys, and hardly a day went by without a fight. Some times their father lost patience at the disruptions and dismissed Gregor back to his goatherding with an exasperated kick. No one was sad to see him go, yet it hurt Georgette to see how young he looked as he slouched off alone.

Every morning Georgette threw the slops from their breakfast to the sow, Bess. Bess's piglets squealed so hysterically whenever Georgette lifted them to estimate their weight that she expected Bess to protest, but Bess took no notice and continued to root in the pottage spilled on the floor. Perhaps, Georgette reflected, she remembered from previous litters that her piglets would disappear as soon as they were large enough to sell in the village market, so she had decided not to love them too much. Georgette didn't know much about the feelings of mothers, although she pictured her own mother in

Heaven almost every night before she feel asleep. She imagined her mother had looked just like the statue of Jesus's mother in the village church, even down to the blue dress.

There wasn't any time to imagine in the mornings. Georgette had to draw water from the well in the village square and scrub their single iron pot, then return home to weed around the beans, leeks and onions in their little kitchen garden, bake enough bread for the following few days, and cook a stew for the evening meal. She cleaned the hut, sweeping the trodden-earth floor with a worn straw besom and putting the straw mattresses outside to freshen on sunny days.

Then she hurried down the hill to the priest's house, where she repeated most of these tasks. Except that Father David had little appetite as he grew older, and the food she made for him lasted more days than it should have. Georgette urged him to eat more, but he said old men had small stomachs, digestion was not easy for him, and he wanted no more than the good bread she baked and a mug of boiled buttermilk. When the villagers brought him food, he thanked the giver kindly but more and more often he sent Georgette to take the provisions to a village family that had been disappointed in the harvest or to a woman still weak from a difficult birth.

As his eyes grew dim with age, weakened by years of close study, Georgette began to read aloud to him whatever he chose to hear. On the occasions when he needed to write a letter, she would sit alongside him at the trestle table, her goose quill frequently dipping into the inkhorn, repeating his words back as she wrote them in small, neat script.

Late afternoon was the time Georgette loved best. Together they would sip warmed, spiced wine and Father David would slip off his wooden shoes, lean back against the rough wall behind his bench and close his eyes. Then he told her stories, exciting stories about Hildegard of Bingen and Heloise, and Georgette glowed with pride and interest in these great women who served the Church as well as any man. Heloise was Georgette's romantic favourite, because Heloise continued to love Abelard, her husband and teacher, even after each of them had taken vows of celibacy. But Father David disapproved of the nun's love letters to the monk. Abelard and Heloise had pledged to be married only to the Church, he pointed out. Vows to the Church – even very difficult vows, he repeated – had to be kept at all costs.

Before dusk, Georgette set out Father David's dinner and hurried back up the hill to stir the embers of the fire and reheat the simple food in her own home in time for the return of her father and brother. Sometimes she would ask about the wheat harvest or the availability of sweet grass for the sheep and goats, but the menfolk answered in short sentences and there was usually silence as they sat on a bench at the trestle table, wreathed in smoke from the hearth, eating hungrily and downing mugs of cheap raisin wine. After their meal, Gregor and his father wiped their greasy mouths with their sleeves, but Georgette had learned from the priest to use a small piece of flax cloth and she wished her men would do the same. She knew better than to take the knives and spoons they had used and wash them thoroughly, as the priest had taught her. Her father and brother would have looked at her in amazement: hadn't they already licked and wiped their utensils clean?

Bedtime came early, after Georgette had done some sewing by the light of the tallow candle, while her father and brother relaxed by the hearth, occasionally extracting lice from their hair and clothing and tossing them into the fire. Father and son slept on their straw pallets before the glowing red embers, but Georgette had her own bed in an alcove on the far side of the room. She did not mind that the rectangular frame nailed on to two wooden legs was a little too short, nor that the leather stretched across it was badly tanned and a little smelly. Her father had made the bed for her so it was precious.

Lately, Georgette had hung a length of rough linen across the alcove to provide some privacy. She was aware of a new need to be alone with her body, as it changed in ways that both delighted and alarmed her. Only recently a young lout in the village had made a remark as she passed and, although she did not hear what he said, she was startled into understanding by Gregor's roar of anger as he hurled himself at the much bigger boy head first, beating him only because of the surprise of the attack.

The subsequent round was more predictable. After that second bout, Georgette hovered near Gregor with a cloth soaked in healing plants she had gathered and boiled herself. But Gregor wouldn't let her touch his black eye. He grabbed the poultice from her hand roughly, pressed it to his eye himself and strode out of the house towards the dark woods. Georgette looked after him wistfully. She wished they could be friends.

CHAPTER THREE

'Pilgrims! Crusaders! Gathering in the valley below the village.'

The excited voice was Gregor's. Herding his goats not far away, he had watched with an open mouth as hundreds of small figures, far more people than he had ever seen in his life, marching from whence he knew not, began to swarm down from a distant hill towards a meadow outside the village. A large cross, catching the light of the sun, brought comprehension. Shouting loudly, he had raced the protesting animals back to the village at four times their usual pace, in order to alert everyone.

The men were in the fields and were not aware of the excitement, but all the children in the village and many of the women hurried to see the strangers, Georgette and Patrice fleetfooted at the front. Georgette expected to hear great sounds, singing and preaching and shouting the praises of our Lord as they approached the Crusaders, but there was only quiet, a quiet that infected the newcomers so that they hushed their exclamations. A host of dusty small children and dusty big children stood silently in the valley, many hundreds or maybe up to a thousand, facing an outcrop of rocks with a flat top that formed a natural raised stage. *Why are they all so young*, she wondered, *and why so still and unchildlike?*

'Lift me,' she whispered to Gregor. 'Please give me a piggyback.' And with rare agreeableness, he did, crouching low while she jumped on to his back and clutched his shoulders.

Now that she was higher, she could see what was on the raised area: it was a man, kneeling as he faced away from the crowd, kneeling with his hands held high so that everyone could see the large gold cross he grasped. But the cross itself was not nearly as gold as the hair of this man. Georgette had never seen hair like it. Like the flames of a fire, like the petals of a marigold, like spun copper and bronze all in waves anointing his head, his miraculous mane of gold was tilted up to God. He was still and silent. And the children were silent.

The man stood gracefully and turned around slowly and Georgette started. It was not a man, but a mere boy, tall but not older than twelve or thirteen, she guessed. He stood as straight as a prince, his elegant cloak hanging in graceful folds. From side to side he gazed, and the crowd pressed forward, staring at him, waiting for the bewitching boy to speak his first words.

'Oh, Lord Jesus,' he began, in a clear, ringing voice that went to Georgette's soul like the sun to a seedling. She straightened herself as tall as she could while hanging on to Gregor's back. Straight up and tall as possible, to be like that boy, to be like him and with him.

'I ask for Thy blessing on the children of the village of Illiers.'

Georgette ducked her head at his blessing. Never before had she been so proud to be a child from the village of Illiers.

'I ask that you bless them, sweet Lord Jesus, with the wisdom to know Thy Word when it reaches them, that they cast away their games and leave their chores, and bid farewell to their parents, and follow me, Thy faithful servant, to redeem Thy Holy Land from the infidels.'

A breath, a murmur, moved through the crowd. The current brushed them forward, closer, uniting them like a school of fish all heading in the same direction. There was no effort in it, but rather a giving up of effort and a giving in to the words. Suddenly frightened, Georgette glanced at Gregor. His face had altered and was almost handsome in its intentness and focus.

The boy's voice drew Georgette back into its power. It was a musical voice, speaking poetry, not speech, weaving around her emotions like a golden net, steadily drawing her closer to this new apostle, this Fisher of Men.

When the last words had looped to an end, the crowd remained still, suspended in a moment of glory. The boy bowed his head and sank to his knees with perfect grace, and the listeners fell to their knees too.

Georgette slid lightly off Gregor's back and knelt in rapture.

Of course, she thought with a rush of certainty, *it makes sense. Many a time I have heard Father David say that Jesus loves us children the most. So we are the ones He chose to drive out the Muslims and Jews from his Holy Land.*

When the boy rose and the crowd with him, Georgette felt like reaching out to touch him with her fingertips, felt like prostrating herself before him. But, she admonished herself, he was not a god to be worshipped; nay, he was a leader to be followed.

And like a clear underground spring gushing up into the air for the very first time, she felt a tremendous purpose filling her body and her head. She was going to follow him. Leave the whole world that she knew. Leave her family and her comforts and follow God's messenger to save God's land. No matter how far, how hard, how dangerous. Putting pebbles in one's shoes was nothing compared with embarking on such a long and winding journey.

She turned to tell her brother – and met determination blazing in his eyes. He too had made the decision to join the Crusade.

As they returned to their hut, absorbed in their separate thoughts, they met their father in the muddy lane, stooped under the weight of the firewood he had cut in the forest. He grunted in greeting and kept walking, passing ahead of them on the path.

'Father, I am leaving home,' Gregor announced without preamble. His father stopped and straightened his back a little. 'A prophet has arrived in our village this eve. He is leading a crusade to smash the cursed infidels in Jerusalem. And I am going with him.'

Georgette interrupted in dismay at Gregor's bluntness. 'Father, I can explain. A young boy touched by God has gathered an army of children who march behind him in a new crusade. He said that the souls of children free from adult sin shall convert the Muslims and Jews and return Golden Jerusalem to the true believers. I understood from his words that I am called to a holy task. Gregor feels it too. But we will return to you, Father. And with God's blessing.'

Their father turned round and observed them, while Georgette's fingers twisted her apron into a criss-cross of wrinkles. Then he faced home and continued walking as if he had not heard. With deliberate movements, he unloaded his wood at the side of the hut. Choosing three branches, he carried them into the hut and bent down to stuff them into the stove.

Silenced by their father's silence, Georgette and Gregor said nothing until they had all eaten the simple evening meal. Only when he had shovelled the last hunk of bread into his mouth and wiped the gravy off his mouth on to his sleeve did their father speak, as if it had taken all this time to marshal his reaction.

'I cannot tie you to the hut if you wish to go,' he remarked as if talking to himself.

'I'm going,' Gregor stated baldly.

Georgette's father looked at her. She said nothing but something in her face must have convinced him that she too was not to be deterred.

'You are just children. How will you eat? Where will you shelter at night?' he said, ever more practical than emotional.

Tears welled up in Georgette's eyes. She reached out and touched her father's rough sleeve.

'Father, all those in our village who heard Prophet Stephen speak hurried to bring out food for the children he led. Our neighbours asked in return only that when the Crusaders reach the Holy Land – where our Father listens most closely to man's requests – they should pray that this one get well, that one give birth to a live child, and the other one escape his bad fortune. It will be that way all along the road. Our Lord will provide.'

'And the danger?' her father replied. 'There are bandits along the road.'

'I'll kill them, just as I'll kill the Muslims and Jews trespassing in the Holy Land,' Gregor retorted. 'This is my chance to see the world, Father. I will not miss it.'

His father made no protest, but turned away and blew his nose into the corner. When he faced the fire again, his bewildered expression pierced Georgette. *Our Lord will take care of him while we are away*, she reassured herself. *In fact, our Lord will be so glad of our family's service that He may even reward our father with a good harvest this year.*

They stayed up later than usual. Their father was silent, cracking his knuckles repeatedly. Gregor sat on the floor, whittling a cross he intended to dip into the chalky lime at the edge of the pond and carry high as he marched. He had wanted a sword but his father had told him he had no money for such costly items and that he must make do with a sturdy cudgel.

Gregor was furious at being thwarted, and even

angrier when his father gave several small silver coins into Georgette's safe keeping.

'Sew this into the seam of your cape, Georgette. 'Tis all I have, so use it for emergencies only,' he instructed.

'We have no need of money,' Georgette protested, but her father was stubborn. Finally, she took the small cloth into which he had knotted the coins and drew closer to the fire to stitch it into her clothing.

'Look after your sister, Gregor,' their father charged. But his words sounded more like begging than ordering.

'I will be occupied with the boys in fighting,' Gregor retorted. 'I cannot be held back by a crying girl scared of the sight of blood. Why doesn't she stay home and take care of you?'

Georgette was indignant. She was not scared of the sight of blood: indeed, only the previous week she and Patrice had served as Father David's assistants in stitching and dressing the gory wounds of a stray dog. But she was suddenly troubled by Gregor's question – why wasn't she staying with her father? He did need her; it was true. But the journey to save the Promised Land loomed as a mountain over the small hill of her father's desire for a hot meal ready when he returned from his labour. He would manage alone; she knew he could manage. And as for taking care of Father David, why, she was sure he would be honoured to lend her to a crusade for beloved

Jesus Christ. And women from the village could help him with his meals while she was away.

Very early the next morning, Georgette packed the things she would take with her on her journey. There was not much. She placed in the centre of her horsehair blanket a sharpened table knife, the spoon her father had carved from horn for her, a wooden bowl, a ceramic drinking vessel, wrapped well in green leaves, a woollen hat her mother had worn, and a second linen smock. She knotted the blanket into a carrying bag, placed it by the door along with her thick sheepskin cape, and hurried to Father David.

She found him in the church, on his knees in front of the *prie-Dieu*, his head bowed over his hands. His back was slumped, and it seemed as if his morning devotion would not end soon. Georgette didn't want to disturb him but if she did not hurry, the others might leave without her.

'Father David,' she began, feeling shy for the first time with this gentle old man.

He turned round slowly, his body looking slight and frail in the voluminous black cassock. 'Georgette?' he asked. 'My eyes cannot see thee for the light shining around your head. Is it you, my child, so early in the morn?'

''Tis I, indeed. No doubt you have heard about the Crusaders who halted overnight outside our village. That is why I did not come to you yesterday. Their leader is a young man, Father David, but a great one. I leave with him today on the Crusade,' she announced, pride in her voice. 'I tarry only for your blessing.'

Unexpectedly, a look of dismay, even horror, swept across his face. She halted uncertainly. Why didn't he open his arms to her and bless her with pride and pleasure?

'My child,' he began, but suddenly he closed his eyes, bent his head and prayed intensely but too softly for Georgette to hear. Georgette watched in bewilderment as tears began to roll down his cheeks and his hands fought against each other, left hand wringing against right hand, and right against left.

At last, he made the sign of the cross, opened his eyes, wiped his cheeks with the sleeve of his cassock and stood up with difficulty. Raising his hands, he laid them gently on her head. 'The Mother Church has ordered support for these Crusades,' he whispered, 'so I bless you and commend you, my child. But I beg Jesus to keep you from harm. Harm to your body and harm to your soul. Thy will be done. Amen.'

Georgette closed her own eyes as he blessed her. She didn't understand his words. She didn't understand his tears. But the most important thing, the urgent thing, was to get back to the group. She gave her dear, familiar, sweet priest a tight hug, dashed away her own sudden tears and hurried out of his hut for the last time.

By the time the priest finally ceased his prayers, Georgette had taken her Pilgrim's Vow in the village square, smiling happily at her childhood friend Patrice in the group of new recruits. Then she shouldered her bundle and was on her way to Jerusalem.

PART TWO

Faith and Folly

CHAPTER FOUR

By the second morning of the journey, Georgette felt as if she had been a Crusader for a long time. Her felt shoes were poor protection against the rough stones, but hadn't she longed to suffer for our Lord? Indeed, many of the children had no shoes at all. The bare ground was hard to lie on that first night, and all the children suffered from a maddening infestation of lice, but she had been so tired she had fallen asleep anyway.

The sheer number of children marching was overwhelming, but she had stuck close to Gregor and had not been lost once. And she had even seen the leader, Prophet Stephen, ride past her group on a high-stepping white charger fit for a nobleman, encircled by five strong youths on far more ordinary horses. His crown of golden hair set him apart, as did the deference shown to him by the others.

All commands were sent down from Prophet Stephen through the ranks until they were transmitted to the smallest marchers, who looked to be seven or eight years old. Georgette and her brother had been assigned to one of ten groups, each with about fifty children of different ages under the strict orders of an older leader. Her group marched together, sat down to eat together, and slept huddled together for warmth and safety.

Many of the youngsters had formed into groups of friends, walking and eating and sleeping so closely they seemed connected by an invisible web. Georgette was courteous to all and chattered busily with Patrice whenever their separate groups marched alongside, but she felt no strong need for an intimate friend, since she had Mother Mary with her always. And, of course, there was her brother for protection.

Around the fire at night she heard scraps of conversation.

'Yeah, me father was also glad. One less mouth to feed, he told me, and he went off to work without a word of goodbye.'

'Well, at least he didn't beat you,' said another. 'The last time my stepfather whipped me so badly I couldn't stand, I told myself I'd either kill him in his sleep – maybe hit him over the head with a shovel or something – or run away. And then the Prophet came to our village.'

'I was jus' hungry,' one called out, to several shouts of agreement. 'Turnips and water, turnips and water every day this past winter, and not too many turnips at that, mind you.'

Patrice stood squarely with several boys who said they had joined for adventure. 'I'd have followed anyone who offered me a chance to see the world, maybe even the Devil himself,' she declared.

Some of the children looked disapproving. There were certainly a large number who had joined for the love of Christ, but Georgette couldn't tell how many.

Patrice had become a great favourite with many of the younger children. At night, little ones crept from nearby groups to join Patrice's circle before a fire, where she sat with a child in her lap, others draped on her shoulders like furs, and told entrancing stories from Aesop's fables.

'The fox and the grapes!' came an entreaty.

'No, we heard that one last night. The wolf and the crane, please!'

Patrice laughed and hugged and told story after story, until the child in her lap fell asleep and the ones leaning against her shoulders slipped to the ground, their heads drooping with tiredness from the day's long walk.

On Georgette's fourth day, a mounted liveryman from the chateau of a count of Gallardon met the young pilgrims. As he drew up to the leader, he seemed unsure as to whether he should dismount, as he would for a nobleman. Stephen was, after all, a herder of flocks from a small village. But the long-haired youth on his pure-bred stallion looked more like King David than David the shepherd boy, so the emissary sprang to the ground and bowed respectfully.

'My honourable lord wishes to put at the disposal of the holy pilgrims the largest meadow in his estate. My lord himself is unfortunately otherwise occupied with members of his family who are ill, but he has ordered his servants to provide the Crusaders with bread and mead. My lord would be deeply grateful if you would pray for the recovered health of his wife, Lady Marie, and his only son, young Jean Philippe. My lord is sure that the prayers of such pure children as yourselves will find a direct path to God.'

'Do you think he is ordered to start every sentence with "my lord"?' someone whispered into Georgette's ear.

She didn't have to turn to know the identity of the speaker. 'Hush, Patrice,' she begged.

Prophet Stephen graciously turned aside from their path and detoured a little to the proferred meadow. There he said a stirring prayer for the noble boy and the gentle noble lady. As soon as he had finished, the marchers threw themselves down on the soft, dry grass in the meadow, examining their blistered feet and rummaging in their little packs.

The food they were given that night was plentiful, and they ate with gusto. Only the loaves of bread were a little underdone – the servants said the baker had come down with the same malady from which the lady and the heir of the chateau suffered.

The Crusaders slept well and the mood among them was good in the morning. It became even better after matins, when Prophet Stephen held up his hand for quiet.

'Today shall be a rest day for us all,' Stephen announced, with a winning smile. 'The count has invited us to remain for another day, to rest our bodies and to repeat our prayers for his family.'

Shouts rang out. 'Hurray for the count!'

'Georgette!' Patrice called. 'There's a stream below the meadow. Come along!'

How good it was to trail sore feet in the cool water and gather early strawberries in the woods. Georgette took the opportunity to wash her muddy smock, spreading it out on warm rocks to dry.

'Keep a good lookout, Patrice!' she warned. 'You're dozing instead of watching to see if any boys are coming near.'

'And so what if they saw you without a shift on,' Patrice retorted lazily. 'What they haven't seen before, they won't recognise.'

Patrice could be infuriating, heedless to the commands of both God and man. But Georgette had known her since childhood, had seen her weep as they carried that bleeding stray dog to Father David, had watched little children drawn into her radius like ducklings to their mother.

That night many of the children seemed listless during Patrice's storytelling and they did not sleep as well as they had the first night. In the darkness, there was a restless wave of tossing and turning, blankets pushed aside and pulled back close.

The next morning, the leader of Georgette's group returned from the daily meeting of all group leaders and reported, 'We're not the only ones to have fever among our members. Some in the other groups are too weak to rise. The Prophet says we will remain here another day to allow the sick ones to rest.'

An hour or two later, the sounds of splashing in the stream and games on the meadow were interrupted by a piercing wail. A spindly young boy, his skin burning to the touch, had suddenly convulsed several times and died. His twin sister, plump and sturdy, shrieked again and again.

'I want my mama! Papa, come and get us!' She clutched her twin's body with hysterical determination, and would not let go.

All gaiety was forgotten, everyone gathered for the funeral. Some of the new Crusaders cried, but those who had been marching for a few weeks simply got on with the job of digging the grave and burying the body.

Prophet Stephen's oration at the graveside uplifted and soothed everyone's spirits. His voice swooped and thrilled as he exalted the dead young boy, a martyr to the faith, an example to all Christendom, surely already a saint at the side of the Lord. The Crusaders sang a rousing hymn. Slowly, the light little body, wrapped in cloth, was lowered into the hastily dug hole, and the travellers waited only for Prophet Stephen's final blessing before dispersing.

There was a shout from one of the older girls.

'Look! Two black flags on the chateau tower. The lady and her son have died.'

Everyone turned to stare at the funereal banners trailing from the stone walls of the castle, announcing a double death among the noble folk. Whispers snaked through the crowd.

'That makes three deaths now. And the cook is ailing too.'

'We have been drawn into a house of plague.'

'Who else among us has been infected with this disease?'

Georgette pushed her way to Gregor's side. He was white-faced at the news but certainly healthy, and he took her hand in his own, an exceedingly rare touch that made her eyes moist with tears.

She was in need of comfort. The next death followed as the sun reached its height, and the next two after that. Soon Prophet Stephen could not preside at all the funerals, and he deputised leaders to bury any in their own groups who died, while he passed like a comforting angel from sickbed to graveside. When he began the *Pater Noster*, he kept a young priest at his side to chant the Latin. But when he spoke his own words, his tongue was as silver as mercury.

'We suffer, Lord Jesus, and we are glad to suffer.
We die, Lord Jesus, and we are glad to die.
For you suffered and you died for us.

Here in this black meadow
There is light.
Your light illuminates our hearts.

We are fortunate to be chosen
for this opportunity
To prove our love for You.'

Patrice didn't have much patience for prayers. She quickly enlisted Georgette as one of her band of roving caregivers.

'Find someone who is alone; sit by him or her. Bring water if the child can sip. If he's cold, cover him with his blanket. If he's hot, wet a cloth and lay it on his forehead.'

Scattered across the broad meadow, sweating children lay calling for their mothers or shivering until their teeth chattered, while siblings or helpers held their hands and sobbed at the cessation of breath.

The count's personal physician was busy with a growing number of patients in the castle but sent his assistant, who was of no use at all, making things worse by blabbering that there was no treatment for this kind of fever and all who fell ill would surely die, and soon. With cold authority, Prophet Stephen ordered the assistant, a number of years his senior, to leave the holy group of children, whose pure souls could defeat death with the power of prayer.

Georgette prayed fervently. She woke up with words of prayer already forming on her lips; she fell asleep beseeching Mother Mary to hover through the night by the side of those who were delirious with fever. In between, she muttered prayers to herself as she carried water from the stream or helped some of the older girls to clean unconscious patients. When they vomited and defecated where they lay, she had to drag them to another patch of grass, wipe them clean, and rinse their blankets and their underclothing in the river. It was best to concentrate on well-known prayers at those times, to distract the mind.

That day, and the next, and the next, the nightmare continued, shrieks and wails indicating a new death, followed by the sound of shovels digging and digging. But many of the Crusaders did not join in the work that had to be done. Some kept their distance, crouching alone among the trees or on the banks of the stream, fear dilating their eyes whenever someone came near.

Georgette's ever-present worry was for Gregor, and she kept her eye on him as he dug holes in the dry earth, slamming his shovel into the clods with a violence that was either anger or terror. But when she saw the tall figure of Prophet Stephen pacing through the camp, his lips moving in prayer, her fear lessened, and she whispered simply, 'Take care of us, Jesus,' and returned to her work.

Jesus took care of them and by the end of the week, the infection had run its course. No one else fell ill. More than fifty young Crusaders were dead, most of them the youngest and weakest in their groups. On top of the fresh little graves, the disturbed soil gleamed blood red in the morning sun.

'You look . . . different,' Gregor grunted to his sister. Georgette did not reply. She felt years older.

Three days after the last child died, when those who were still weak could manage to walk with support, the young Crusaders rose early to leave the sad place. There was angry rumbling over a suspicion that the count had lured them to the valley of death, hoping God would heed their prayers to save his own kin. Several of them spat in the direction of the chateau.

As they left the lord's rich farmlands, they found themselves marching through thick forests, unclaimed and untamed. The narrow path was cleared only as wide across as required by a cart and horse, so that at most three or four children could walk abreast on it. Others in the large and unruly procession scrambled up the banks into the trees, tripping frequently on the uneven ground, over roots and brambles. Many times they would slip on the slimy moss and fall, standing up again with streaks of damp earth on their legs and arms. The younger ones cried and were either consoled by older siblings or had to wipe away the mud and tears on their own and struggle on.

When they finally halted for the night in a clearing, the Crusaders huddled dispiritedly in their groups, struggling to light fires with green wood, and unsatisfied by the half-portion of lukewarm turnip soup doled out by the group leaders. The provisions that the grief-stricken count had provided for their onward journey disappeared rapidly when simmered into soup for so many mouths.

'Why only half a bowl tonight?' demanded Gregor. Georgette shrank behind him. Couldn't Gregor just take what was given? She wished he would be quiet.

'Not enough for everyone,' the leader grunted shortly.

'But you have a full bowl,' Gregor remarked.

The leader flushed with anger. 'Prophet Stephen told the leaders to take double because they work harder, keeping the groups together,' he replied. He stood like a bull or a stag ready to fight, his legs planted apart, his head jutting forward aggressively.

Gregor scowled and opened his mouth to retort. But the dominance of the leader was palpable, and Gregor turned away with a muttered oath.

That night many of the travellers coughed and moaned in their sleep. The earth was moist and cold under the thick canopy of firs and pines and oaks. Curled in her damp blanket, Georgette dreamed she was buried under the dark ground, chilled to the bone. In her dream, she opened her lips to pray but clods of the clay surrounding her fell into her mouth. Coughing and spluttering, she woke herself up and lay shivering in the blackness.

In the morning, they emerged from the cool forest and marched across a large swathe of land where the trees had been felled. The sun rising high behind them warmed their backs and heads, and their clothes steamed as they dried. Georgette thought she could see, maybe even touch, the holiness hovering above the innocents like morning mist.

Prophet Stephen knew when the children needed inspiration to raise their spirits. He sent song leaders from group to group, teaching Crusader anthems about Jerusalem, about the golden stones, the sacred ground, the holy hills. In each group there was at least one youngster who played the curved shepherd's pipe – a ram's horn that had long outlived its original owner – and at least one other banging on a drum or blowing the reedy shawm, which was Georgette's favourite. Those without instruments could pick up two sticks and saw them together to create a musical accompaniment.

The sweet music was a salve and to Georgette a stimulant. How glorious, she exulted, as the high clear voices rose heavenward. Hour after hour they sang the Crusader anthems interspersed with nursery rhymes, traditional rounds, Christmas carols and even love songs from the May Day feast. They pushed ahead with renewed faith.

The thick forestland had presented another difficulty in addition to uneven footing and dampness. It was not possible to spot human habitations when the trees blocked the view in all directions. But this stretch of cleared ground led them up a gentle hill from which they could see smoke from several chimneys at a distance off to the right. Prophet Stephen ordered some emissaries to ride ahead and request that the villagers prepare food for the holy Crusaders.

Soon the astonished but pious and hospitable villagers were donating the last of their winter reserves to feed the hungry crowd of children. When the procession arrived, soup was bubbling in cauldrons over huge fires and baskets overflowed with wrinkled apples from the previous autumn. Georgette and Patrice caught sight of each other through the crowd and Georgette laughed to see Patrice's mimicking of a dog licking her lips in anticipation of food. Although it was not yet time for the noon meal, they all fell to and ate heartily. Afterwards, the boys were dispatched to catch salmon in the river and hunt pheasants in the woods.

That night they had permission to sleep in a fallow hayfield at the furthest reaches of the village. The ground was scattered with old straw, sweet and dusty, and the Crusaders slept like the babies many of them were.

When they resumed their march the next day, a number of children and youths from their host village joined their ranks.

CHAPTER FIVE

The villages were more numerous and sat closer together as they neared the city of Paris. The spires of Paris were so tall they first saw them when they were still a day's walk away.

Georgette could not believe she and the other ragged and dirty travellers were to enter the great capital.

'The King of France will receive us in his palace,' Gregor asserted. 'He will recognise that we are brave Crusaders, despite our age.'

Prophet Stephen had sent a messenger ahead to request an audience with King Philippe Auguste, as well as food and a space to settle for a few nights. When the messenger returned, Prophet Stephen met with him privately before ordering the leaders of the groups to make an announcement to each band.

'The King of France, Philippe Auguste, has graciously granted an audience to our Prophet. Tomorrow morning, in St Denis, Prophet Stephen will enter the presence of the King.'

There was whispering in the crowd. The presence of the King.

'But the King says there is no open space in Paris large enough to accommodate so many children. He orders us to settle on the large meadow outside the city walls, on the banks of the Seine. Food will be provided by the royal palace and the people of Paris.'

Groans of disappointment unsettled the air. Georgette exhaled slowly. Surely she would never again be so close to the famous city.

'Like wild dogs, he keeps us outside the gates,' Gregor growled. 'We're good enough to enter Jerusalem, but not his precious Paris. A curse on him – may his one good eye suffer like the other.'

'Oh, Gregor,' Georgette said. 'Perhaps the King is worried we will catch diseases in the city. Patrice has heard that the wife and son of the count in Gallardon were in Paris shortly before they returned home and became ill. Cities are places of disease and dirt, they say.'

Gregor swore. He was in no mood to be placated. He was hungry and tired and now angry too.

Food helped, as it always did. The bread baked in the King's own kitchens and delivered by the curious gatekeepers in relays was comfortingly warm and fresh.

The stew was rich with fatty meat and the mead was sweet. They slept well that night, the city's walls looming impressive and dark above them.

In the morning, they took the opportunity of bathing in the Seine, choosing a place as far away as possible from the open canals that drained into the river from under the walls, churning with the refuse of the good citizens of the city. Georgette helped to bathe the younger children and washed both her and Gregor's underclothes. Sunlight glittered on tall buildings within the city, just out of their reach.

When Prophet Stephen returned from his royal audience in St Denis, several hundred new recruits followed him. The experienced Crusaders roared with approval and gathered close to hear him talk. They had fed and rested their bodies and were ready for the Spirit now.

Prophet Stephen's handsome face glowed and his eyes were feverishly bright as he held aloft a new and even larger gold cross presented to him by Queen Ingeborg. A red silk banner with yellow flames fluttered in the breeze, a copy of the sacred *oriflamme* presented in times of war by the Abbot of St Denis to the royal leader. King Philippe Auguste had received him, Stephen, God's humble shepherd boy, briefly but with due honour.

'King Philippe has sent the following message to us all,' he announced. He motioned to the shy and unprepossessing priest who led them in prime and vespers every day. The young man stepped to Stephen's side and struggled awkwardly to break the great lump of sealing wax on a ribbon tied around a rolled sheet of parchment. It finally broke open and fragments of red wax flew into the crowd, pursued by scampering children eager for souvenirs. The Prophet's lieutenants shoved the children back to their places none too gently and then the priest read aloud.

'I, Philippe Auguste of Paris, King of France, do bless in the name of God the children who march to Jerusalem in His name. May He protect them in their blessed innocence and crown their pilgrimage with triumphant success. I proclaim that this procession be called the Children's Crusade and that it shall be known and honoured throughout my fair land. I order my subjects along the way to open their hearts and their food stores to these pilgrims. May the Holy Spirit be with His children. In the name of Jesus Christ.'

There was another roar of approval from the crowd as the priest finished. Prophet Stephen raised his arms to Heaven, prayed for the good health of Philippe Auguste, and preached eloquently about the greatness of kings as representatives of God on earth.

Gregor immediately forgot the insult that had infuriated him earlier. 'King Philippe Auguste himself praises our holy Crusade,' he whispered, as proud as if he himself had been awarded royal approval.

The Prophet was concluding his address. 'Harken well. Today it is the King who is blessing us. When we reach holy Jerusalem, we will ask the Lord's blessing on the King.'

'We will be the ones to bless the King,' Gregor repeated with satisfaction.

That night, their second in the meadow outside the city gates, the bread was not as fresh, the stew had been replaced by broth, and the mead was in short supply. Gregor's mood swung again.

'His Royal Highness is too fine to speak plainly, but he is showing us with his food that we have worn out our welcome and should move on,' he remarked. 'One day of hospitality and he is done with us.'

The next day they turned their backs on the walls of the big city and took to the road again. Patrice came to walk with them a while, and Gregor and Georgette asked if she knew what route they were taking. Patrice was an excellent source of information. Her brain spilled questions and soaked up answers.

'We are on our way to Vendôme,' she answered.

Gregor looked blank, but Georgette tried to picture the map of France that Father David had shown her.

Patrice explained, 'Prophet Stephen is going back the way he came when he left his own village, Cloyes.

Vendôme is the nearest city to Cloyes, and that was where he first preached and gathered crowds. There were many children who wanted to join him, but he told them to gather in Vendôme and await his return from an audience with the King.' Then Patrice brightened as she had an idea. 'Maybe the citizens there will be so glad to see us that there will be lots of food.'

A Crusader who had gone ahead returned at a gallop, his face alight with excitement and his words almost unintelligible. Word of Prophet Stephen had spread throughout the region. There were so many awaiting the Prophet that he had not been able to count them, so many that they could not fit in the town square and had decamped to an open meeting place outside the city gates.

Gregor and Georgette turned to each other in silent amazement as they came within sight of Vendôme. Possibly two thousand children and youths were standing with their bundles and their crosses in the grassy meadow. They roared with excitement and might have mobbed Stephen if he had not spurred his horse into a gallop, thundered a circle around the entire crowd in triumph, and eventually halted on a raised point, where he began preaching. Instantly, the huge crowd became silent.

He was so beautiful, Georgette marvelled. His body was long and lean and perfect, his hair was a miracle, a sign from God that he had been chosen. He shone with a light that drew her irresistibly. Did the first Christians feel this powerful call when they listened to Jesus's Sermon on the Mount?

The crowd shifted slightly and she caught sight of Patrice. Patrice was looking in another direction, whispering to a girl beside her as she pointed to whatever she could see of Vendôme above the city walls. She was not listening to Stephen at all. This was just another stop on an adventure for Patrice, Georgette realised.

Whether their hearts were full of God or wanderlust, the Crusaders left Vendôme the next day as a small army rather than a large crowd.

Now there were about thirty groups of a hundred Crusaders each. The pace of the journey slowed to a slouch and it was near impossible to find enough food for all.

It happened that they marched for two days without anything at all to eat. On the third morning, Georgette woke up with her stomach aching. In her past life she had never had abundant food to eat, but neither had she ever been truly hungry. It was strange how much her stomach felt like a separate living thing, growling and rumbling, tightening in occasional, painful spasms. She felt squeezed flat, like an empty sheep bladder with the air sucked out.

The boys killed a boar and several deer before noon, but the soup that resulted, divided among so many, contained only a mouthful of meat for each child. That was the only food they had, plus acorns and berries they found along the way, some of which caused diarrhoea and vomiting. Patrice came by to tell Georgette that some boys in her group were chewing on bark and reporting it to be not as inedible as expected, but she admitted she had not tried it herself yet. The younger children cried inconsolably that long third day.

As she lay down at dusk, Georgette heard the sounds of a child retching, coming from behind a bush. Rising wearily to her feet, she called out reassuringly and walked over to help. A girl of about eight years was stuffing earth into her mouth, bits of grass and tiny stones included. As Georgette approached, she vomited up the whole mess, but no sooner was her mouth empty than she thrust more earth into it. Saliva and bile dripped from her chin. Her eyes were wide and overly bright. When she noticed Georgette, she scampered further into the bushes, disappearing from view.

'Like a creature of the wild,' Georgette whispered, willing herself not to retch at the very sight.

The next day it was discovered that a number of the youngest children in Georgette's group had died in the night, whether from hunger or exhaustion or some illness their bodies were too weak to fight.

The others stood staring at the tiny piles of cloth, skin and bones.

'Come on now. They have to be buried before we move on,' the leader said. 'They are small enough that we can put them together in one grave.' He picked up a shovel and marked a spot. 'Boys, start digging here.'

None of the youths moved.

'I am weak,' one muttered.

'I need my strength just to keep walking,' another begged.

The leader shouted and ordered and pleaded, but the boys averted their eyes. Finally, the leader threw down his shovel. That was the first time they left their dead in a shallow ditch, covered only lightly with soil and piles of old leaves.

The wild beasts will eat them tonight, Georgette thought, as she lashed together some sticks to make a cross for the makeshift grave. *And perhaps 'tis fitting. In this terrible hunger we have become more like animals than humans.*

The group that marched on was sombre and gaunt.

CHAPTER SIX

The marchers had to have at least the promise of food ahead, or they would lie down from weakness and die in the hundreds. Prophet Stephen sent off four youths on horseback, each in a slightly different direction, to search for any prospect of a meal. The crowd stumbled on listlessly in the hope of good news, resting frequently, prodded by their leaders to get up again and keep moving forwards.

Just as dusk fell, one of the scouts returned in energetic triumph, riding like a boy who had recently eaten his fill, astride a horse with sweet hay in its belly. The large and prosperous Abbey of Blois was less than two hours' march away, and the abbot had undertaken to feed the holy Crusaders in the morning.

The scout related how he had been taken to a cavernous kitchen and plied with food by the monks. 'The head cooks are twins,' he went on, 'such jolly fellows and as alike as two peas in a pod. They insisted on giving me seconds of everything and they –'

'Enough about the cooks,' Prophet Stephen snapped. 'Spread the word among the Crusaders that tomorrow we will have a breakfast fit for a king . . . or an abbot.'

The children received the news with relief, but the night was long. The next morning they covered the distance to the abbey as quickly as they were able.

Even the huge refectory where the monks ate every day was not big enough to seat so many, so thirty feeding stations had been set up on the grassy slope outside the abbey. Each one was manned by a monk standing behind a massive cauldron of porridge. The twin cooks were red-eyed from sleeplessness, having cooked through the night for their huge group of guests. But their smiles were broad as they moved from group to group, chortling at the hungry children whose grimy faces were barely visible behind the bowls raised to their mouths. There was enough for a second serving for each, but most of the Crusaders could not cram any more into their shrunken stomachs.

After they had eaten, the abbot led tierce outside rather than in the abbey so that they could all hear. He was an impressive man, intense and ascetic in looks, with a commanding, precise voice that carried across the slope. Their stomachs heavy, the Crusaders listened contentedly, but thought their own leader much more handsome as he stood confidently beside the stern abbot. Stephen had taken to wearing a peacock feather in his hat, and the sun danced in the iridescent turquoise plume.

After tierce the children rested in the sun on the slope, devoured fresh bread and a thick bean soup in the evening, and slept well through the night. The next morning they resumed their march after breakfast.

The jolly cooks had prepared vast quantities of food for their journey. They were made recklessly generous by their personal interest in a new recruit to the Crusade from their very own abbey. He was a tall boy, quiet and serious, wearing a new black hood that he repeatedly pulled forward to cover his face.

CHAPTER SEVEN

In the seven years that followed his removal as a child to the Abbey of Blois, Robert had almost no contact with other children. Instead of being mocked for his unblinking seriousness, he was now required to study and to assist his new guardian in his writing for up to twelve hours each day, interrupted only by meals and the routine of the Divine Office. He quickly adjusted to waking like the monks at 2 a.m. for the matins service followed by the lauds service. After a little sleep, he woke again at dawn to begin the day with the prime service. Then his duties began, punctuated by the services of tierce, then sext, then none, and ending on most days with vespers before dark. Sometimes the abbot needed him to take dictation after dinner, before compline. Only then was he free of work, but it was bedtime almost immediately. It always seemed he had just fallen asleep when he was woken at 2 a.m. to start again with matins. Through all those years, the abbot's highest praise was a thin smile, and so Robert was proud when he earned that concession.

If he had a rare moment of free time, he loved to talk to the diverse travellers who stayed overnight in the abbey. They laughed at the boy's eager questions, then marvelled at his quick grasp of the things they told him, from details of political intrigue to the scientific principles used to invent such useful things as hoists, and the great advantages of the Hindu numerals, brought to Europe by Arab traders and renamed Arabic numerals.

'Now go and play, boy,' one traveller finally ordered him. 'At this rate, your brain will wear out before you are a man. Do you not know how to play at fencing or shoot at birds with a bow and arrow?'

Robert did not know how to play, but fortunately his intense mental world was relieved by two individuals whom the abbot did not deign to notice. The only adults who had ever shown him affection were near the bottom rung in the abbey: the jovial cooks in the monastery kitchen, Brother Puck and Brother Peter. These twins were uncomplicatedly devoted to each other and to their work. They loved food, whether cooking or eating it, and they loved God. What better work could they find in the world than to cook huge meals every day for the monastic servants of God?

Middle-aged and round, they were comically

identical, except that one had a scar from a burn on his right hand. Robert looked carefully at each cook's hand before looking into his face whenever they met, and gradually he learned to distinguish mischievous, forgetful Brother Puck from steadier Brother Peter. Robert was by far the youngest boy living in the abbey and the kind cooks quickly made him their pet.

'Psst, young Robert!' Brother Puck would hiss. 'Come to the kitchen when you can slip away from your lessons.'

Looking around to make sure that Abbot Benedict was nowhere in sight, Robert would dart into the kitchen and crouch under the chefs' long trestle table. He waited. The sneaking of treats by the twins had its own sweet ritual.

After a few minutes, Brother Puck would exclaim animatedly, 'Is that a rat next to the stove?' or 'I think I smell burning – check the bread!'

While the assistant cooks were distracted, a spicy little sugar-almond cake or a bit of salted herring would be thrust under the table by Brother Peter, and Robert would seize it and pop it into his mouth.

Chewing rapturously, he admired Brother Puck's creativity in coming up with new distractions. When he had wiped his mouth and his hands on his breeches, he expressed his appreciation silently by patting the two pairs of worn comfy slippers peeping under the table. Then he hurried back to Abbot Benedict.

'Jesus forgive us for leading the boy astray,' Brother Peter would mutter uneasily, but Brother Puck had no qualms.

'And who else but we two adds anything sweet to that lad's day?' he demanded. 'He studies so hard and learns so fast you'd think the abbot would give him a little treat occasionally or even a word of praise. But have you ever seen him smile at the boy? Have you?' And Brother Peter was forced to admit he had never observed the abbot's grim visage softened by a genuine smile.

During the first five years, Abbot Benedict kept Robert near him almost all the time, even during the night hours, with Robert sleeping on a straw pallet at the foot of the abbot's plank bed. But as the abbot's feverish ambition made him less and less able to sleep through the night, he decided that the slight sounds of breathing from Robert might be contributing to his insomnia, and so Robert was assigned his own cell, adjoining that of his master. He even had his own oil lamp, an earthenware dish filled with water on which the oil and wick floated. The abbot gave it to him with instructions to continue his studies in the night if he was unable to sleep and observations on the sinfulness of wasting oil and wicks unnecessarily. It was the only thing his guardian had ever given the boy, and thus it was precious.

By this time, Robert was nearly twelve. He had not realised while he lived in the abbot's cell how much he needed to have some time alone with his thoughts, pacing if he wished without being reprimanded, away from constant observation and shaping. For the first time, the boy, previously all mind, began to explore his heart. Feelings of any kind were frowned upon by the abbot, and Robert had had little chance to recognise his own. But with the luxury of hours alone in a room of his own, he began to think about . . . himself.

He wasted little time wondering who his parents were. The only past that he could remember was an early childhood of loneliness, humiliation and hunger. He preferred to forget what was over and done with. The future held some great deed in which he would glorify God. Of that he was as sure as any young boy imagining the future.

It was the present that absorbed almost all his emotions. He felt increasingly constrained by his guardian's relentless supervision. He endured waves of resentment at the man's peremptory commands and demands at all hours of the day or night. At these times, his childhood habit of self-restraint helped him to keep his reaction well below the surface. But he promised himself repeatedly that in the years to come he would find a way to end the dependence he hated.

It was soon after Robert turned twelve that the abbot announced the boy was to accompany him on a trip to Paris.

Robert's eyes opened wide with delight but the abbot cautioned him. 'This is not a mere jaunt, Robert. I have been honoured with an invitation from a member of the standing council of judges, a distinguished jurist who wishes to discuss my writings on canon law.'

The abbot's pale cheeks flushed a faint tinge of pink as he made this announcement, and Robert stared at him in wonder. Was that pleasure in the abbot's face? 'You are old enough now to accompany me and be of service.'

'Yes, Père Abbé,' Robert murmured, subduing his excitement until he was out of the abbot's sight and scurrying to the kitchen to confide in Brother Puck and Brother Peter. He had seen nothing of the world but a small church in a small town and the confines of a large but quiet abbey. Now he was to see Paris. The cooks were gratifyingly impressed; they too had never travelled farther than the few miles of the journey from their home village to the abbey.

Robert's journey was one of great disappointment and then great satisfaction. As they approached the gates of the city, the carriage driver pulled to the side unexpectedly and stepped down to inform the abbot that a messenger had signalled him to halt and wished to speak with the abbot. The message was that the distinguished judge was ill and there was suspicion that the sickness from which he suffered might be no ordinary ague, but the plague. Until further notice, the abbot was advised not to approach him for fear of infection.

Robert felt tears of disappointment filling his eyes. He blinked rapidly to get rid of them.

Coldly, the abbot ordered the messenger to wait, in case his services were needed, and retreated into silence while he calculated his next move. The setback was a terrible pity. He had spent many sleepless hours practising about what he should say in the coming meeting. Rumours he had heard led him to believe that he would be invited to join the standing council as an advisory assistant to King Philippe Auguste's ecclesiastical courts, a prospect that was much to his taste. He had reached the position of abbot at an unusually young age and after a decade at Blois he was eager to move into a position that would offer him more ... intellectual stimulation was the way he would phrase it, a position that would afford him more power and influence than he could hope to wield in an abbey in the countryside.

In the past year, during those sleepless nights, an original idea to increase his ranking among equals, a way to stand out in the minds of his superiors, had taken hold and he was eager to begin. The idea had grown from his rigidly concealed pride in the extraordinary intelligence of his protégé, pupil and young companion, the slight boy sitting opposite him, whose eyes were blinking furiously to hold back tears, an effort the bishop fully expected him to make. The curiosity that had led him to take on the freakishly clever orphan had expanded into a calculating ownership. If he could show off, in one or two significant chambers of the great beehive of the church, his discernment in adopting this particular orphan rather than any other street urchin and the dramatic results of his disciplined system of education, then his unusual achievement, with its obvious emotional appeal, might bring his name more vividly to mind for advancement than those of competitors. He lay awake choreographing subtle ways to display the boy's prowess. When the invitation to a meeting with an esteemed jurist in Paris had arrived, he was ready.

Now, at fever pitch, although none would have recognised it from watching him, he felt extremely reluctant to return to the abbey and wait for a repeat invitation. And what if the judge did not recover, and another judge lost no time putting forward a different name, for reasons easy to imagine? No, the abbot should waste no time in pursuing a new opportunity to display his unique young asset.

After a period of reflection, his face cleared and he summoned the messenger to the window of the carriage.

'Carry my compliments to the rector of l'université de Paris,' he instructed, his voice perfectly controlled. 'Inform him of the circumstances that have forced me to change my plans for this visit to Paris, and request that I may take advantage of his past invitations to stay as his guest and witness the great learning taking place there. Return quickly with a reply.'

The messenger bowed his thanks for the coins dropped into his hands and galloped off towards the city gates.

'Close the shutters,' the abbot ordered to the carriage driver. 'If there is indeed plague in the city, we should not be exposed to the ill air.'

Robert swallowed as the shutters slammed shut like the door of a jail. How he had looked forward eagerly to the sights of great Paris. And now he was sealed in a stuffy box waiting with the preoccupied abbot.

Neither of them noticed the other's sigh of relief when the sweating messenger returned with a courteous invitation from the rector. The world brightened, although the shutters stayed closed and Robert saw nothing until the carriage drew to a halt.

Springing out to assist his master, Robert found himself in a large walled courtyard surrounded by handsome buildings with Latin mottoes carved over their entrance doors. Young men in long black gowns of a cut he had never seen before were walking from building to building or sitting on stone benches, talking intently, laughing easily.

'Those are the students who study at this great school,' the abbot told him.

'But are they not too old for school, Père Abbé?' Robert asked in puzzlement.

The abbot's lips lengthened in what passed for a smile. 'They have learned all that a children's school can teach them, Robert. This is a school for advanced students, where the brightest young minds of Europe can study theology, law, medicine.'

'And then . . . ?' breathed Robert.

'Why, they may become Masters of Theology or perhaps Masters of Law . . . but hush, a messenger approaches.'

A student led them to the rector of the university,

who welcomed them courteously and ordered refreshments for the travellers. Robert sniffed unobtrusively at the aromas that wafted from the goblet he was handed. Back at the monastery, the abbot's drink of choice, offered only when he was feeling especially satisfied with some advancement of his career goals, was a non-alcoholic brew of green apples and blackberries, sour and austere as the abbot himself. This sweet liquid boasted of grapes and sunshine and honey. Sipping slowly, Robert sat on a bench slightly behind the abbot and listened attentively as the two men discussed church business. It seemed to him there was a subtle element of competition in the conversation. Each professed the greatest respect for the other, but went on smoothly to mention an influential connection or recent accomplishment of his own. It was like the dances at court that a travelling minstrel had once described to the young boy: the apparent coming together followed by a drawing away, the show of modesty before the showing off.

Musing, he was startled when the abbot indicated him, Robert, with a gesture of his head and said, 'For example, my protégé here, young Robert, was an illiterate foundling whom I adopted and have educated in the strictest tradition. I have made no concession to the modern prattle about permitting students to question and challenge. At the tender age of twelve, he is now fluent enough with canon law to serve as my secretary in drafting an initial response to vexing issues that come to my attention – drafts I improve upon, of course. Many a time I have been gratified by the results of my didactic methods, for this is my first experience educating one so young, you know.'

The rector turned to Robert, observed the shy youngster with the long ragged scar marking his face, and spoke to him in a deliberately simplified Latin, 'Are you familiar with some of our great scholars, child?'

Robert did not need the abbot's meaningful look to rise to the occasion.

In the Latin of Ovid and Virgil, he murmured that he was greatly in the debt of the abbot for introducing him to the admirable clarity of Gratian's code of canon law and the classic theological discussions in Lombard's *Sentences*. He even added his regret that the Paris council's ban on the study of Aristotle's *Metaphysics* would prevent him from humbly begging to know the opinion of the rector on the controversial work of the great ancient.

'Impressive,' the rector acknowledged. 'Perhaps we shall see your young protégé at our university in the future, Abbot Benedict.'

'That would be an honour to us both, Rector,' the

abbot feinted. 'Although I believe he could join the class of second- or even third-year students, perhaps, as his grounding is excellent.'

'We shall see, shall we not, Abbot Benedict?' the rector parried.

The two men fell into a theological discussion, and Robert listened intently. Then, without warning, the rector turned to the boy.

'Young Robert of Blois, behind that tapestry is a private passage leading directly to our university library. Hasten and bring me the book with Abelard's views on this matter.'

Then he turned smoothly to the abbot and resumed their conversation. It would have been humiliating for Robert to interrupt and ask more precisely which of Abelard's books the rector required. The abbot cast a worried glance in his direction. But Robert murmured his assent and slipped behind the tapestry. A winding stone passageway, with slits near the top of the wall that let in a little light, led him to a small door. There was a key in the keyhole and it turned easily. In a moment, Robert was in the great hall, lined with wide armaria. Their doors had been removed for convenience, and the manuscripts and scrolls on the shelves were displayed in an orderly fashion. There were also chests of different sizes and styles, standing on their sides with the lids open like doors to reveal more manuscripts. Rows of sloping lecterns at chest height bore heavy codices, which were invitingly open for study but were chained to the lecterns for fear of theft. Robert inhaled the aroma of parchment, cured leather and dust; to him this was Heaven.

Then he realised with dismay that the large room was empty of any librarian, student or monk who might help him find what he needed. He stood still and concentrated on his task, looking down at the mosaic floor to avoid being distracted by the riches surrounding him. Yes, he was quite sure. There were two books, not one, by Abelard that discussed the subject the men were debating. It would look well if he managed to find both of them.

Had Robert been educated in an abbey with fewer manuscripts, he would have been daunted by the grandeur and breadth of this great library. There were, he estimated, perhaps seven or eight hundred books in the *armaria*, without counting those in the chests. But Abbot Benedict had built up a formidable collection of almost a hundred books in his own library at the abbey, using taxes wrung from the farmers who rented abbey farmlands. Robert had spent many hours in that room, almost as much time as he spent in the abbot's cell and certainly more time than he spent alone in his own.

Robert moved briskly from shelf to shelf, opening one book on each. Once he had roughly grasped the classifications used by the librarian, he was able to narrow his search. He was glowing with pride as he hurried towards the little door, carrying both works.

At that moment, he heard from the other side of the main doors the sounds made by a key in a heavy lock – no, two keys in two heavy locks. He froze, and was momentarily blinded by a shaft of sunshine as a tall man pushed open the heavy doors and entered. Like the rector, the man wore a fancier variation of the strange gowns worn by the students out in the entrance courtyard.

Agitated dust motes whirled in the stream of light as a stern voice demanded, 'How did you get into the library, boy? What are you doing with those manuscripts?'

The glow of pride turned to a blush of embarrassment and shyness. Looking down at his feet, Robert stammered an explanation.

The man turned to look at the little door, which was ajar, and turned back to stare at him. 'You found what the rector needs without any assistance?'

Robert ventured a quick glance at the man, who, he now realised, must be the librarian. What a wonderful job. Oh, fortunate man.

He nodded.

The librarian looked at him thoughtfully. Then he said, 'Go straight back to the rector and take care not to drop your valuable load.'

Robert disappeared through the little door, remembering to lock it behind him, and soon emerged from behind the tapestry like a magician.

The abbot's subtle sigh of relief was more precious to Robert than the rector's exclamation of surprise and approval of his selection.

'The precentor was at prayers? The library was empty?' the rector asked.

Robert nodded.

'Yes, I knew it would be thus, and I did not expect you to bring back even one correct book on your own, boy. And so rapidly.' He clapped Robert on the back and turned to the abbot. 'You have my sincere congratulations.'

From that point, the rector was eager to show Robert all the wonders and achievements of the university. The atmosphere was tense, with the rector clearly interested in Robert alone and the abbot campaigning repeatedly for praise of his own success in pedagogy. Along the tour, Robert saw more to delight him than another of his age would see in the trove of a peddler, but he knew well that he must turn repeatedly to his master to acknowledge the abbot's claims. After years of only the occasional, brief word of praise from the abbot, he found the rector's attentions excessive and distracting. Would that he could have wandered this extraordinary place alone, for as long as he wished.

The dramatic presentation of Robert's abilities turned out to be only the first of a number of similar experiences. The abbot had decided the time was ripe to harness his prodigy's brilliance to reflect glory on himself. He invited important guests to the abbey and drew the conversation repeatedly to the success of his foray into education, introducing Robert as 'a foundling plucked from the streets of Tours'. Robert was at first surprised but obliging; however, eventually he began to feel uncomfortable and resentful as his feats of memorisation and analysis were paraded.

He shows me off as if I were a dog that can do tricks, Robert fumed to himself. *Only God is responsible for whatever I am able to do with my brain. But he demands the credit.*

As unconfident as he had been before, so did he become overly confident now, silently building pictures of his wildly successful future. But again and again Abbot Benedict slapped him to earth with a stinging rebuke. The abbot was more driven than ever, making the young boy keep the hours he kept himself, giving him lessons instead of letting him sleep between lauds and prime, and sometimes even superseding the rule of the Great Silence to dictate important letters to him after compline, as the candle spluttered. Robert began to feel a new despair. It was impossible to imagine his teacher relinquishing power over his future.

He was trapped in the web of the abbot's ambition.

CHAPTER EIGHT

The abbot was reading edifying stories from *The Lives of Saints* to the monks as they ate dinner in their customary silence in the refectory when he was interrupted.

The twin cooks ushered a youth into the huge stone hall and addressed the abbot in alternating sentences.

'Pardon us for interrupting, Father,' Brother Peter said humbly.

Brother Puck took over eagerly, 'But this young man said it was a matter of urgency.'

Brother Peter explained, 'He says that thousands of holy children are starving in the –'

'Let the boy talk for himself,' the abbot snapped.

The twins thrust the boy forward and flanked him for support. 'Greetings, Father,' he began hesitantly and then he swallowed with difficulty, overwhelmed not so much by his audience of several hundred silent monks but by the bountiful repast they were eating. 'I am . . . I have been sent by . . . I am to request . . .'

He halted and swallowed his saliva again as a plump priest close to him lifted a juicy chicken leg and bit into it with relish.

'Out with it, boy,' Abbot Benedict ordered.

'Begging your pardon, Father,' the boy said, blushing, and told the story in a rush. He was one of a huge crowd of children and youths, who were travelling under the leadership of a shepherd boy from Cloyes who had seen God. God had anointed him Prophet Steven and told him to lead a new crusade to free Jerusalem from the infidels. It was to be a crusade of pure hearts, a crusade of children. King Philippe Auguste himself had received the Prophet Stephen in Saint Denis and had given his blessing to the Children's Crusade, before sending them on their blessed way.

Now the young Crusaders were halted a short way from the monastery, in sore need of food and rest. He had been sent ahead to find good Christians who could give them shelter. 'And food,' he added.

The abbot pointed to the bottom end of the table at the far side of the hall. 'Sit there and eat.'

The boy wasted no time obeying.

Abbot Benedict turned to Robert, who sat as always on his left, slightly behind him. He curled his lip in a sarcastic smile. 'These babes and toddlers dream of freeing the Holy Land where grown men in armour have failed? Perhaps we should seize the misleading charlatan who has aroused them and lock him in a monastery cell to learn true Christianity, and tell the others to go back home before they get a well-deserved whipping.'

'But the King has blessed –' protested Robert.

'Don't be an idiot, Robert. Have I not spoken to you many times about the machinations of politics? His Majesty is already concerned about the lack of grain available in Paris after the bad harvest. He would not want thousands of children with empty bellies making demands on the city's reserves. That must be why he met the leader not in Paris but in St Denis. Of course, he gave the so-called "Crusade" his blessing – it would not be politic to give them a curse. Then he rapidly sent them out of his way, towards Jerusalem – but also towards us.'

Robert was silent. Every cynical word was probably correct, but his imagination was caught by the image of a visionary young leader accompanied by a long procession of innocent children dressed in white. In his mind's picture, the hero was about his own height and build; indeed, the hero was much like himself but without a disfiguring scar.

Abbot Benedict sourly ordered that preparations be made to feed the crowd in the morning. Likely the pilgrims would start walking towards the monastery at first light and arrive after sunrise, too late for prime. He gave Robert permission to delay his secretarial tasks the next day in order to help. The abbot himself was not to be bothered until they were fed, then he would lead tierce outdoors for monks and Crusaders together.

Early the next day, Robert was feeding the fires under the cauldrons of boiling porridge, the rising steam mixing with the morning mist, when he heard a shout in the distance. He turned to see the silhouette of a young boy on horseback at the crest of the nearby low hill over-looking the abbey.

The youth halted his charger and surveyed the valley, his erect body and crown of curls framed against the new blue sky. His horse reared slightly in impatience and he controlled it perfectly with one gloved hand. His long black cloak draped elegantly over the flanks of his white stallion but was open at the front to reveal the scarlet cross glowing on his chest. In his free hand, a tall golden crucifix flashed in the first light like a magic wand.

Robert's breath caught. A group of older boys galloped to his side and followed his example by pull-ing up dramatically. Then the first Crusaders came into view along the crest of the hill, hundreds – nay, thou-sands – of small plodding figures, most in ragged clothes. The leader, conscious perhaps of eyes watching from the abbey, held still, the morning sun outlining him in a dramatic golden aura. Then he raised his sparkling crucifix to the heavens and led his followers down the hill.

Robert's thoughts swirled feverishly as he served food to the ravenous travellers. But his eyes never left their leader, whom he now saw was younger than himself and – to judge by his salutation when the abbot emerged – uneducated.

How does he lead them all? How did he inspire them to follow him? What might he accomplish with this prodigious mission? The questions tumbled and beat in his head. And most pressing of all, the one that ached inside him, was *why?* Why had God chosen this precocious farm boy, when he himself had dreamed of being chosen by Jesus to do something great in the service of God that would ever be remembered. He, Robert, had been given the gift of brilliance. He had been educated in Greek, Latin, church doctrine, church history, papal protocol, philosophy, mathematics and even a little medicine. No shepherd boy could know as much. *Why not me, my Lord? Why did You choose him?*

The young leader requested the monastery's hospitality for a full day and night of rest, and the abbot assented, though without warmth. Robert helped serve the pilgrims a light midday meal of bread and cheese and mead, and a supper of hot, filling soup. Then he begged to be excused from attending vespers and compline, telling the abbot quite truthfully that he had a bad headache, and retreated early to his cell.

He lay on his hard cot, the rough blanket discarded on the stone floor, his intense grey eyes turned to the pulsating stars beyond the window of his cell, praying as he had never done before.

As the hours passed, the stars' mysterious signals seemed to grow clearer. It occurred to him that his life had been leading to this point, that Jesus had directed his steps – his childhood, his adoption, his education – for this exact purpose. He was to pace within the narrow cloisters of the abbey no longer. He, Robert, was surely meant to join the Crusade.

Robert's decision was the first major choice he had made in his life, and he made it with startling certainty.

After matins and lauds, he asked permission to enter the cell of the abbot.

'Père Abbé,' he began.

The abbot raised his cool eyes from the letter he was reading.

'I ask permission to join the young Crusaders when they depart our abbey,' Robert said, a sudden unnatural calm causing him to talk as evenly as if he were asking permission to take a walk.

The abbot's eyes narrowed perceptibly. He spoke briefly and definitely, 'Your work is here, at my side. You will not go.' He turned his attention back to his reading.

But his young acolyte stood firm.

'I have considered my path, Père Abbé, and I believe Jesus Christ wants me to join this Crusade,' Robert said. 'I hope to return safely to you and our work here, but if I die along the way, I will have been of service to the Lord in a different way.'

The abbot turned to look at him again. The circumstance was extraordinary. Never before in their long and unvarying relationship had the boy disregarded any word that came from his lips. He opened his mouth to strip the boy of his insolence with one harsh sentence, to make him creep back to his proper place, cringing and contrite. But he held still and his brow furrowed in calculation.

Robert's own eyes watered but he did not withdraw them from the long stare. His mind was made up. Jesus had a reason for wanting him, Robert, to join this crusade. And he would do so.

If Robert were more honest with himself, he would have recognised another reason – one that was less exalted – for his need to join the Crusaders. He was jealous of the Prophet, consumed with envy. This farm boy had shown him up to be a dreamer rather than a doer.

And yet he had to be near Stephen. He had to take the opportunity of observing the charismatic leader and learning the secret of his powerful energy, if he were ever to grow into his own destiny.

The abbot chided himself for not being prepared for the boy's first sign of independence. He was already fourteen, and overdue for this rebellion. The older man briefly considered ordering Robert to abandon his idea forthwith, locking him in his cell, if necessary, until that band of silly children and their peacock of a leader were far away.

The boy's set face brought his thoughts to heel. The abbot had observed Robert closely since he was a little boy of seven. He had watched the boy pray for long periods, ignoring the pain of kneeling on the cold hard floor. He had seen him keep up manfully with the hard physical labour performed by young monks. He had heard the young child refusing the blandishments of the jolly cooks in order to return to his work in the library. Like a silent black shadow, the abbot had watched and observed and overheard. He knew there was no chance of changing Robert's mind. This was a boy who would not break the faith, however he interpreted it should be read.

The abbot was startled to realise how much he would miss the boy's company. He was well aware, and told himself it didn't bother him at all, that there was not another human being in the world who would not consider it harsh punishment to remain in the abbot's presence hour after hour. And even if some were willing, he, of course, would not be satisfied with the company of anyone less exceptional than himself . . . and the boy.

From habit, the abbot turned to his perennial preoccupation. What could he gain from this situation, from young Robert's ungrateful but unbreakable decision? Could he turn it to his credit that his protégé, whose exceptional intelligence he had proclaimed in high places, was to join a holy crusade? Robert would be allowed to wear the blue cross, signifying the considerable status of a returned Crusader, on his return to the abbot's side. They would look well together, the abbot in the robes of a member of the Ecclesiastic Council followed closely by Robert bearing the striking blue cross, experienced and matured on his return.

That is, if he returned. The abbot briefly considered the prospect of the boy's death along the road, but dismissed it from his mind. Our Lord would not take the young life that had been carefully and brilliantly moulded by the abbot in His service. The abbot's years of training that exceptional brain, guiding that strong character, could not go in vain.

A wry thought almost brought a smile to his blood-less lips. The boy had convinced him, Abbot of Blois, to change his mind, truly a rare feat. What remarkable powers of persuasion Robert would have as an adult, as the abbot's right-hand man and perhaps even as his confidant.

Of course, it would not do to show the boy that he had been allowed to make his own decision. Speaking for the first time in long minutes, the abbot said, 'You are dismissed. Remain in your cell until prime while I pray for guidance on this matter.'

It was fortunate that the abbot's prayers were answered in the next hour or two, and that he received the same direction from Jesus that his student claimed. There was even time for him to write a short letter to his superiors with the news that he had enrolled his beloved and brilliant young protégé in the glorious service of the Holy Crusades and to humbly beg them to pray for a successful journey and the boy's safe return to the service of the Church.

Before proceeding outside to lead prime for the Crusaders, he entered the boy's cell and, not acknowledging the travelling stick made ready with a small bag knotted to its end, gave Robert permission to join the Crusade. He also gave a puzzled assent to the boy's request to take with him the little earthenware dish that had held oil, water and a wick. He had no memory of giving the lamp to Robert.

He commended the boy to Prophet Stephen's care, oblivious to Robert's discomfort at the implication of the authority held by the unchildlike child leader, and making it clear to observers that Robert's new direction had been his guardian's plan all along. This was confirmed by the handsomely bound breviary and the overly generous gift of money that he presented formally to Robert for his travels, with a brief speech in front of the gathered monks of the abbey.

The Prophet was impatient to return to the road and there was no time for long farewells. Robert accepted the blessings of the assembled monks with some embarrassment. The jolly twin cooks burst into tears, hugging him between them like a morsel of beef between two loaves and weeping unashamedly on each other's rounded shoulders and Robert's thin ones.

That was the only time that Robert needed to summon his resolve. For almost eight years he had been content within the walls of the monastery, now he left without turning around, his steps light, long and quick.

CHAPTER NINE

The first days outside the monastery for Robert were an assault on his entire being. Unused to children, he was suddenly jostled by an uncountable number of them. At night, the discomfort of being exposed to the elements was far less than the discomfort of the consciousness of bodies moving and breathing, snoring, coughing and sometimes crying, all around him.

During the day there was no place to be alone. At the abbey, there were strict rules about bodily privacy, and the abbot frowned on any of the monks hawking and spitting or blowing their noses on to the ground. Here children and youths defecated in full view, evacuated the mucus from their noses in whichever way was most convenient, and commented – at least among the boys – on each other's genitals and the girls' breasts. He had pictured his fellow travellers as pure young Crusaders.

Although he was already fourteen, and thus one of the older members of the Crusade, he was filled with his old fear of being tormented by other children before Abbot Benedict removed him to the abbey. Within days, he was universally and openly called Abbé because of the black hood he wore day and night, shading his face from full view and keeping his ropy scar a secret. But his remoteness put paid to plans of either persecution or friendship, and soon the members of his group turned to better sport, leaving him alone.

Finding himself truly unobserved, Robert became the observer. As he watched a group of boys play leapfrog, the littlest one alternately weeping with frustration and laughing with abandon, the others forming and breaking alliances by the minute, he remembered the last time he had seen such antics:

These children act like the litter of kittens that the twin cooks once kept in a corner of the kitchen, he thought.

His greatest interest was in the Prophet Stephen, but it was not easy to get close to him physically. During the day, the leader rode with his favoured youths on horseback some distance ahead of the straggling, slow-moving crowd. At night, they settled in the choicest spot, sat around a roaring fire built for them by youngsters from other groups, and ate and drank without restraint. The toughest-looking boys guarded Stephen against any pestering approaches.

One night, Robert managed to draw quite close to their circle, crouching in the shelter of bushes nearby until they fell asleep, watching silently and catching whatever words of conversation he could hear. Stephen himself seldom spoke, but when he did throw in a comment, there were roars of laughter, although Robert had not understood any joke in the words. There was little about God and the soul in their discussion, it seemed. Robert crept away unsatisfied.

After he had been two weeks on the road, everything changed. A mounted messenger trotted up to Robert's group and conferred briefly with the group leader.

'Robert of Blois,' the leader called, 'our leader Stephen has need of your services. Go with this man.'

Robert froze.

'Come,' the messenger urged impatiently. 'Get up behind me. It's a long way to the front group.'

'I don't know how,' Robert murmured. 'I've never ridden on a horse.' There was a shout of laughter from a group of farm boys who had been listening to this interchange. Here was a member of their own group summoned to meet with the Prophet himself, yet he could not even climb into a saddle.

Within seconds, they had hoisted Robert up behind the messenger. His legs hung down awkwardly and he clung to the waist of his guide. He was very far from the ground.

'Godspeed,' his young grooms called good-naturedly. 'Be careful the horse doesn't take a bite of your boot!'

The horse was urged into a canter and Robert went pale with fear. He was bounced high and hard with every movement. The road, the bushes, the children they were passing were a blur, and his fingers tightened on the messenger's girdle, squeezing the fold of thick material as if it were paper. He knew he was going to fall; it was just a matter of how long he could hold on.

But soon the horse slowed to a jolting trot and came to a stop. Clumsily, Robert slipped to the ground. He had not had a chance to ponder the inexplicable summons by the leader.

Stephen sprawled on a rich cloak in the centre of his group of lieutenants, talking and laughing while his followers laughed even louder. Eating titbits from a bowl of salted salmon, he left Robert standing for a few minutes before turning to him.

'Do you know the service for dawn?' he asked without preliminary.

'Yes,' Robert answered, remembering a similar question asked of him by the abbot one fateful morning in Tours.

'And evensong too?'

'Yes,' said Robert again.

Stephen looked at him with undisguised surprise.

'How old are you? How did you learn everything? They're long.'

Robert could not resist. 'It was easy. I'm fourteen now but I've known prime and vespers since I was six.'

There were a few low whistles.

'I told you I saw him saying every word by heart while the abbot of his abbey was leading,' boasted one of the youths.

'I need you to lead the Divine Office from tomorrow on,' Stephen announced with command, rather than request or invitation, in his voice. 'Only the morning prayers and evensong – we don't have time for the others.'

'I'm not an ordained priest,' Robert protested.

'I'm not worried about that,' Stephen announced airily. 'We don't have any other choice. One of the priests died of fever and the other told me today that he is unable to continue with us on the morrow. He has a crippling pain in his back, he says. *Bah*, too old, I told him. This is a crusade for strong young people.'

He waved commandingly at Robert. 'I'm told everyone calls you Abbé. Well, that's convenient. You look the role. You know the words of the play. Now you are the official abbé.'

He laughed and turned to the messenger. 'Get his blanket and pack and bring them here to our group.'

As the youth cantered off, Stephen pointed his finger at Robert. 'Sit,' he ordered, and returned to his conversation.

Robert sat.

It was very pleasurable, Robert soon found, to have young people looking at him with respect, moving out of his way, asking him to bless them as if he were a real priest. Of course, he did not give blessings or lead Mass – that would be against church law – but he had decided that it would be appropriate for him to recite lauds and vespers if there was no priest to do it. He found he was modulating his voice, throwing it out to the group, noting approvingly his own fluency and clear enunciation.

The days seemed sweet, riding high with the older boys through the countryside in the warmth of spring. Although his cowl still shadowed his face day and night, he felt a new confidence in his stance. He even practised initiating a few brief conversations with young girls. They responded eagerly and courteously and he turned away, flushed with success.

All the while, he watched the Prophet carefully, relishing the opportunity to observe more closely.

The time to learn how Stephen worked his magic was very specific. When the Prophet was preparing to address a large crowd, he ordered his lieutenants to leave him alone and sat a little way off with his back to the crowd, his legs sprawled casually, holding his cross strangely, as though it were a shepherd's staff. Sometimes he lay on his back, shading his face with his hand.

When he rose, he was clearly in an exalted state. His eyes glittered, brilliant and hypnotic. His sermons were passionately inspiring, in a rhythmic and poetic style that played the emotions like a maestro. His voice was an instrument of God – caressing, furious, consoling, rumbling, even screaming, then suddenly so low it purred but could be heard everywhere. When he stood tall, his arms raised, begging – nay, ordering – God's blessing on them all, his golden halo reached heavenwards. When he paced in a small space, he turned abruptly in a low pouncing movement that drew swooning sighs from the girls. Charismatic creature, great cat, holy angel.

New recruits continued to join at almost every village they passed, few of them older than adolescents, most much younger. Thousands of children marched, prayed, ate and slept without adult organisation or restraints, led only by a group of boys of whom the oldest was barely eighteen, selected by a twelve-year-old prophet. This alone was a miracle.

But Robert's novel and enjoyable position as one of those privileged leaders did not blind him to the dramatic difference in Stephen when he was released from the extraordinary fervour of his preaching. Stephen was truly a devoted servant of Christ – when he was filled, miraculously, with the Spirit. But when he was not preaching to his flock, Robert was astounded to realise that the Prophet was a master manipulator, shrewd, lazy and conceited. He enjoyed food with his lieutenants before others were served and he never went hungry. He beguiled his chosen youths, permitting them to take care of his every need as if he were bestowing generous favours. He played them off against one another, and then turned remote and cruel overnight, rejecting their fawning praises with no explanation. Not once in private did he speak of Jesus or the Church, not once did he give any hint of a desire for spiritual growth in himself or others.

Robert spoke very little among Stephen's group, and no one noticed his observant attention. He had a role and a purpose, and he was paid with inclusion, not respect. He learned the limits of that equation during his first meal with the group. As the bowls of pottage were being filled around the group's fire, Robert coughed, opened his breviary to lend himself some gravitas, and offered, 'Shall I lead us in grace before we begin our meal?'

There was a sudden quiet. The boys turned enquiringly to Stephen. Lounging on his side, Stephen reached out a languid arm, grabbed a hunk of bread and stuffed it into his mouth. He laughed in Robert's face, exaggerating his open-mouthed chewing. The other boys nearly fell into the fire with hilarity, rolling like puppies on the grass.

Robert pulled his hood down further and tried to shrink into himself. The group quickly lost interest, but it was a while before he dared to serve himself, and he said grace silently. Reaching into his pack for his horn spoon, his finger was cut by something sharp. The messenger who brought his pack from his old group had dumped it carelessly from the horse to the ground, and his clay lamp was smashed.

A punishment that serves you right, he told himself, licking a little blood from the finger. *'Tis a sin to refrain from acknowledging Christ. You told the abbot this Crusade would lead you closer to God. Take care that your weakness does not send your soul on a journey to Hell instead.*

Angry at himself, he was angrier at Stephen. But the anger contained a kernel of gratification. The young Prophet's apparent perfection, his dramatic channelling of God's word, had shaken Robert's sustaining faith in a precocious greatness within himself. Now there was a secret pleasure in uncovering feet of clay. If Stephen turned out to be ranked lower before God, didn't that mean his own rank was higher?

One night Robert was present for a conversation around Stephen's fire in which the boys boasted in gory detail about what they would do to the first Muslims and Jews they found. As the beer flowed, Stephen and his henchmen competed with one another to think of the cruellest torture methods.

Disgust and revulsion rose like bile in Robert's throat as he slipped away from the oblivious group to pace in the dark forest.

'O God, true General of our Crusade,' he prayed, 'surely Your beloved son would not want these false Christians as His soldiers? Yet they too believe they have been chosen by Thee, that they do Thy will. How can we ever know Your will with certainty?'

Robert had been alone all his life, yet he had never felt as alone as he did among those young people gathered together in the name of Jesus Christ.

Prophet Stephen preached less often as the weeks passed. He was roused to his charismatic state of prophecy only when they reached towns that were substantial enough to provide a worthwhile number of new Crusaders. He was hardly seen in the ranks during the daily march.

But in the evenings, as the groups of one hundred sat around their fires, he could be glimpsed wandering from gathering to gathering along with his two closest lieutenants, never approaching close to any circle but watching from a slight distance, his hypnotic eyes slipping from face to face, sometimes making a quiet comment to which the other boys replied with approval and low laughter. Each of them carried a handsomely tooled leather flask and took frequent sips.

Robert was unable to get close enough to hear what was being said, but he noticed that sometimes one of the boys would crouch behind one of the girls and whisper a few words to her. The girl seemed startled, but each time the chosen one stood up and followed the older boy obediently into the darkness beyond the circle of fire. The boy would return in a few minutes, and go off with his friend to the Prophet's fire. But the girl was not with him. Nor was the Prophet.

The same thing happened almost every night, although never twice in the same group. Some of the girls looked defiant, even proud, as they slipped back to the group, long after everyone else was sleep. Most looked shaken and disoriented. One of them wept for a long time, and Robert stumbled away before she could hear his own sobs at her shame and distress. It was clear to him now. The girls were always pretty. The Prophet was nowhere to be seen while the girls were away. Robert writhed against the knowledge. He ground his teeth in helplessness.

Charlatan! he would accuse Prophet Stephen silently whenever the boy preached. *False idol! Antichrist!* he would hiss at night when he could not sleep.

The worst was that, when he tried to pray for help, he could not find words of humble beseeching, only violent curses the likes of which had never come to his lips before.

He shuddered. He was losing his faith and without it he would be lost entirely. The abyss before him was bottomless.

And yet he did not leave. He could have taken up his bundle, fallen behind his group and begun the walk in the opposite direction, back to the abbey. Any of the Crusaders could have left the Crusade at any time. But very few did. Was his reason the same as theirs: that the Prophet Stephen exerted a powerful fascination, a magnetism that was almost impossible to resist? Or was it that Robert was curious to see how it all ended? He could not believe that this fake Moses would actually lead them to the Promised Land, yet there was always a slight possibility and that was too tempting to give up.

And what if I did leave the Crusade, he thought. *I have nowhere to go but back to my old life.* He pictured the small world of the monastery and the looming figure of the abbot. *Nothing will change until I die of old age within those stone walls*, he despaired.

CHAPTER TEN

Late one afternoon, they passed a large village. On the far side of a village pond, the small rough houses were like those in any village, with poor children who stared at them with wondering eyes and a few women who looked as if they had never had enough food to give one beggar, never mind a crowd of thousands. But on the side of the pond closest to the road stood a sizeable cluster of blackened, ruined wooden huts, closely interspersed with a few stone houses that appeared almost undamaged but deserted. The sight was curious. Clearly the stone houses had withstood a big fire on this side of the pond. But where were the people who owned them? Why was the village almost empty?

An older boy passing from the back to the front of the group overheard their speculations and tossed them an explanation. 'Those stone houses are not empty. The Jews inside are hiding because Crusaders have passed through here before and put their side of the town to fire.'

'Jews,' they murmured, and the word spread through the crowd. They could see now that the remaining houses had barricaded doors and shuttered windows. But the wooden huts were burned beyond repair, including what must have been a very tall building in the centre.

What had the Jews done to the Crusaders to have their houses destroyed, Georgette wondered. Patrice would know, but in this great crowd, it had become difficult for the girls to find each other for a chat. Perhaps the Jews had tried to stop the Crusaders from marching to Jerusalem. Well, they had been put through a terrible scare and would learn not to create difficulties again. What evil people they must have been to have persecuted gentle Jesus, who brought them the laws of loving others as oneself. And their wickedness seemed not to have ceased, she mused.

Soon the travellers settled for the night in a field of yellow mustard flowers, glorious under the setting sun. Georgette felt uneasy at being so close to the village of the Jews during the night. She imagined malevolent eyes peering out at her from between the cracks of houses or barns.

Some of the older boys lounging around the fire were also thinking about the Jews nearby.

'There cannot be many left,' one said. 'A dozen of us with stout sticks could wedge open a window and haul out the sinners. We'd torture them until they swear to take up the True Faith.'

'All Jews are moneylenders,' another boy told everyone. 'My father said they take advantage of good Christians in trouble.'

'Loaning money and charging interest is forbidden by the Lord,' someone reminded them.

'So let's take back their ill-gotten gains,' came the eager response. 'It is for our sacred cause.'

With such temptation at hand, a dozen sturdy farm boys stole off into the darkness, heading back towards the village they had seen earlier. In their midst, enthusiastically swinging a thick tree branch as a makeshift cudgel, was Gregor.

The big brass bell was rung to summon all to vespers around the largest communal fire and Georgette was swept along with the crowd. Her mouth chanted automatically the well-known words and she sang mechanically too, but in her mind she was picturing her brother and the other boys chiselling open those few houses and dragging out the infidels in order to show them the light.

The boys had been excited about this early opportunity to be true Crusaders. Gregor's eyes had glittered. Such action would suit his angry nature, she reflected.

This was probably exactly what he had pictured when he volunteered for the Crusade.

The boys returned very late. Georgette hadn't been able to sleep, despite her weariness, and she hurried to serve them from the cauldron of pottage still hanging from a tripod above the glowing coals of the fire. The biggest one, who seemed to have appointed himself their leader, swaggered over to the fire and bade her hurry.

'Hungry from a good night's work, eh, boys?' he called out.

The same boy ate first and began the story of their adventure first.

'We managed to prise our way into two of the stone houses,' he began. 'There was an old man with his woman huddled in one, and parents with three Jewish brats in the other.

'We started with the old man. Dragged him outside, and his wife too, and pulled off his smock and breeches. You should have seen him standing there naked, the old frog. But he wouldn't acknowledge Jesus as the Lord, no matter how much we hit and kicked him. Why, I pulled so hard on his disgusting long yellowed beard that big chunks of it came out in my hand.

'Then the father of the three children left his family and rushed at me. Oh, we gave him a good beating. How dare he touch a Christian with his unclean hands? We hit him with our sticks from all sides –'

'– and when he fell down we kicked him again and again,' interjected another boy.

'He didn't give in, even when we all piled on, but when his children and wife ran up and screamed and cried, he stopped struggling and said he would do what we wanted.'

'What did you want him to do?' one of the younger children asked, wide-eyed.

'Well, we made him kneel –'

'Hah, we grabbed his hair and pulled him from the ground to his knees, the heretic!'

'– and we made him pray to Jesus.'

'At first he hesitated, as if we were teaching him the Devil's own words,' interjected another big boy.

The leader took back the story, 'So I helped by punching him before each word. It was funny – first we gave him a word, then I punched hard, then the wife and children screamed, then he repeated the word. All the way through an entire Hail Mary.'

'Did the old woman cry?'

'Nah, her eyes were closed all the time and she was praying in their strange Jewish tongue. So I slapped her really hard and she fell to the ground. She shut up after that.'

Georgette's stomach heaved. She glanced question-ingly at Gregor. He had been silent throughout the tell-ing and would not look at her now. His pottage was untouched. Suddenly, he stumbled to his feet and went off alone to sleep.

Another boy left early too. He was not one who had gone on the expedition, but the tall and quiet boy who led the hours. When he had heard the part about the Hail Mary and the beating, he slipped away into the woods, where his dark form was lost among the trees. Georgette thought she heard vomiting, but maybe she was mistaken. The laughing around the fire was loud and excessive, almost hysterical.

When they started marching again the next day, Gregor seemed to edge away every time Georgette approached him. And indeed she was not sure what she was going to say to him. She certainly couldn't ask him the questions she had been asking Jesus every waking hour since she had heard the boys' account of their adventure.

She decided to leave Gregor alone and let him work out his mood on his own. That method had always worked at home, but this mood was a strange one. It wasn't that he seemed angry. In fact, Gregor had acted this way only once before that she could remember, and it took her a while to recollect the occasion. It was when she and Patrice had found the bleeding stray dog. That was the dog she had helped Father David to stitch up, earning praise for her steadiness. Meanwhile, Gregor had shrunk from contact with her in just this kind of way. Later he had surprised her by asking if the dog would be all right. In fact, he seemed to know of the dog's wounds before she told him.

This time it took two long days until he sought her out. One morning, he fell back to walk beside her on the stony road, and in silent agreement, both of them edged off to the side a little so that they could talk unheard. His face was blotchy and unhealthy, and there were black shadows under his eyes.

'What ails you, Gregor?' she asked.

It took a while for him to reply.

'I helped beat up that Jew man,' he said.

As Georgette raised her eyes to his, he added defensively, 'That was the only way we could get him to pray to Jesus.'

He went on,

'It was when he was repeating the Hail Mary. I beat him with a cudgel for hesitating, and when he finally finished it, he stared straight at me with the strangest look. I think he cast a spell on me. I have been feeling poorly ever since.'

Georgette had no words to reply. They walked on silently, and they did not speak about that night again.

Gregor had caught a chill during the damp cool nights and he continued to feel poorly over the next several days. He had little appetite and he tired easily. At night, a deep, hacking cough kept him awake and left him weak and sore. He was not alone in his illness. Many of the Crusaders coughed persistently throughout the night, one setting off the others until they sounded like a discordant brass chorus. Georgette tried to keep him warm and hand-fed him hot broth, but nothing she did seemed to help.

After four days, Patrice appeared at her side, disobeying her exasperated group leader's command to stop her gallivanting and remain with her group at all times. She had heard of Gregor's ill health through another child from their home village, and she had begged an old crone they passed on the road for a few sprigs of tansy and chamomile. Georgette remembered Father David boiling those herbs into a soothing hot drink for a child who was coughing severely, and she made the brew with haste. But the herbs hadn't worked for that child and they didn't work for Gregor. He coughed so roughly that he spat up thick blood.

Georgette stayed awake at Gregor's side that night, feeding the fire and trying to persuade him to drink the bitter tonic. There was no moon, and the only light came from the twisting red tongues of the fire, writhing and choking on the damp twigs she fed it and smoking constantly, malevolently.

Georgette felt more alone than she had ever been before. She had thought they would all care for one another and crusade as a loving group united in Christ, but that atmosphere had seeped away after the first few days of cold and shortages of food. Now your blanket was as likely to be stolen as a coin lying on a highway, and Georgette saw many older youths who seemed to be using more blankets than they had brought on their journey, while younger ones lay shivering on the spruce boughs they used for bedding, wrapped only in their cloaks.

Fortunately, Gregor still had his blanket from home. She wound her own blanket around him too, but hurriedly loosened and reshaped the wrapping because he resembled a corpse in a shroud. Some time before dawn, his breathing eased and his coughing lessened. Georgette prayed her thanks; the tonic must have helped finally. Now she could rest for a while before the others arose. She lay down close to Gregor, took his hand in hers, and gave way to the exhaustion that was turning her body to lead. She slept.

About three hours later, the bustle of the Crusaders preparing to get on the road again seeped into

Georgette's consciousness. She kept her eyes closed, wanting desperately to sleep on and on and on. When she was little, she used to fall asleep in the afternoons in Father David's hut while he taught the village boys. Wherever she dropped off, under the wooden table, or on a bench in the corner, she would always wake to find herself on soft straw, covered by a warm cape, and the priest would bring her a little milk to drink before she arose. How she wished the kindly old man was near to look after her now, to cover her against the morning cool, and especially to rub her hand, which was numb and sore from remaining in one position for hours. Groaning, she pulled it away, and felt someone's fingers dropping from her own. Heavy. Cold. In an instant she was awake and bending over her brother's chest. There was no movement, and his lips were icy.

A wail tore through the group. 'Mother Mary!' Her head thrown back, arms stretched up to Heaven, Georgette cried out, 'Send him back, Mother Mary! Send my brother back to me!'

The group leader hurried over and put his own ear to Gregor's chest. He forced Gregor's half-open eyes closed and stood again.

'He died a martyr to the Holy Cause,' he pronounced. Turning away, he told some of the older boys to borrow a shovel from whoever had used it last.

'And dig a longer hole than last time,' he ordered them. 'The boy was tall.'

Worse than his rough practicality was the past tense that he used. *Was tall . . . Was tall . . . Was tall*, echoed in Georgette's mind as she threw herself flat across Gregor, clutching his stiff, cold shoulders. She would not let them put him under the ground. It was not possible that he was dead.

A few girls came over to pat her back awkwardly. 'Don't let those boys steal your brother's blanket when they bury him,' one warned, and Georgette wailed louder.

Guilt pressed like a laden pack on her back. Not only had she deserted her father, but she had allowed his only son to die. If she had found the herbs earlier, maybe he would have lived. If she hadn't fallen asleep, maybe she could have shaken him back to life.

Never before had she dwelled in such blackness. The dark earth pulled her powerfully and she wanted to sink down and never rise again.

And then she heard words, not spoken by any human soul, but travelling through her body like warmed cider given to one who is frozen. The words dissolved her pain, covered over her raw wound like a soothing poultice. *Yea, though I walk in the valley of Death, Yet will I fear no evil.*

Georgette felt light and free, as if a hand had removed

an oppressive weight and she was aloft in a foreign atmosphere. Smoothly, in one movement, she rose to her knees, bending her head over her clasped hands. Now she was murmuring, the words emerging from her lips, but the human sound was only a vehicle for enunciating what was pronounced with great love in her head. Her sobbing ceased and she only hiccupped now and again, held in serene rapture.

Two boys came and carried away her brother's body and still she murmured, motionless. The others whispered, but none dared disturb her. The boy in a black cowl who led the hours had been drawn by the anguished wail. Now he stood some way behind Georgette and bowed his own head in the presence of her faith.

When the group's leader summoned her to the new grave, she walked calmly to her brother's brief funeral. She answered 'Amen,' crossed herself, placed a twig sprouting with new leaves on the upturned clods of soil, and joined the Crusaders as they departed.

A few children followed her closely for a while, hoping to witness some manifestation of the Divine after her unusual behaviour at the side of her brother's body, but her face was so ordinary, her manner so humble, that they soon lost interest. Only the one wearing the black cowl continued to follow her, but at a distance.

CHAPTER ELEVEN

As the journey turned into months, the irregularity of food, the exhaustion of continuous travel and the lack of shelter all took their toll.

'Another three slipped away last night,' Patrice informed Georgette one morning. 'They're stupid not to stay with the Crusade. They'll never get home alone.'

'Perhaps they'll find work in a nearby village,' suggested Georgette. She was more concerned about the Crusaders they had been forced to abandon in various villages along the way because they were too weak to walk. Who knew whether the villagers would be kind enough to nurse them back to health?

The original system of organisation was no longer closely observed. Leaders did not recognise all the members of their groups. No one knew how many young Crusaders there were in total. Some said there were one or two thousand. Others swore the number must be higher than five thousand. At times, there was a chaotic lack of supervision and order. Silently, Robert watched the confusion.

By now the Crusaders were travelling through the miles of forests that blanketed the middle of France. Those who remained were toughened by their travels and more experienced in finding food and shelter. They were thin and tired, but their determination burned bright.

In the thick forests, wild boar were a common sight, roaming freely and rooting for acorns in the fallen leaves with loud snuffles and grunts. The boys went off on hunting parties, returning triumphantly with bristly pigs hanging between them on stakes. One day Patrice appeared in the train of the boys, dancing and twirling. There was blood on her hands and forearms and a streak on her face.

Georgette exclaimed, 'Patrice, you look like a . . . like a savage. Where on earth have you been? And where did that blood come from?'

'I went on the hunt!' Patrice boasted. 'The boys said I couldn't, so I followed them secretly until we were too deep into the forest for them to send me home. Then they were glad I was there because I spotted the herd of swine first. It was so exciting!'

She laughed merrily at Georgette's consternation and danced away. Georgette shook her head and hurried to find a clay pot to catch the precious lard that dripped from the pigs over the fire. She mixed it into wheat flour and baked some rough cakes on the glowing coals.

The boys hunted for other wild animals too, especially deer and rabbits, and they fished in the streams and lakes for a welcome change of diet. At night, they told stories around the fires, and stacked low piles of springy boughs from coniferous trees to raise them above the damp ground while they slept.

The Prophet preached on the Sabbath, and sometimes on other days. Georgette's strength was always renewed by his words. It was scarcely believable that she, an ordinary farmer's daughter, was part of the army of Jesus. How fortunate she was.

One night Georgette left the warm fire, going a short way from the group for some privacy. She could never piss or empty her bowels at the side of the road as so many did, especially those sickened by the rampant dysentery among their ranks. Before she returned, she admired the great old oak trees around her, gleaming in the moonlight. She loved the scent of their acorns rotting on the forest floor. *Our pig Bess would enjoy rooting around with her snout here*, she thought, smiling at the image.

A figure loomed suddenly in front of her and she shrieked. She caught a glimpse of the face and realised with shock that it was the leader himself, Stephen, who stood in front of her, directly in front of her.

She was embarrassed at being caught so clearly having just finished pissing. *My skirts were barely down*, she thought and blushed.

Stephen smiled. 'What is your name, girl?' he asked.

'Georgette,' she answered, wondering at his interest.

'So pretty,' he murmured, and Georgette started. Had he really said she was pretty? It wasn't the first time that a boy had told her that, but she hadn't expected their leader, who was chosen by the Lord, to think of such things as a girl's appearance. She shivered.

'You are cold,' Stephen said in that low voice. 'Let me feel how cold your hands are,' and without a chance for her to respond, he took her hands.

Instinctively, Georgette pulled away at what in another boy she would have called impertinence. But his hands only slipped to her wrists and kept hold there. She froze. There was the smell of ale in the air.

'Don't be frightened,' he said to her, smiling again. 'You are with your leader. Aren't you glad I find your face pleasing? Very pleasing . . .'

His hands holding her wrists were strong but Georgette could have broken free if she wished. She had not escaped Gregor's violent tempers many times as a child for naught. But the hold preventing her from breaking away had little to do with Stephen's hands: it emanated from his intense eyes boring into hers, his golden curls lifting and waving like fiery serpents, his voice that sounded thick and deep. He murmured things she hardly heard, crooned words in a stream that took away her will to run. Smooth, soothing words as if he were taming a wild animal. Gently, he released one of his hands, keeping the other firmly around her wrist, and stroked her face with his fingertips, moving slowly downwards, her neck, her throat, her breasts. She trembled violently but his eyes were on her and his voice trapped her. Skilfully, his hand caressed her breasts more and more firmly, burning through her shift.

Suddenly, he stopped and listened. Georgette heard it too. There was loud rustling in the forest very near them. Dry leaves crackled underfoot, a twig snapped and a figure stepped out of the shadows and halted next to them. Georgette saw the tall, quiet boy who always covered his head in a dark hood and prayed in fluent, mellifluous Latin. Staring not at her but at the leader, he stood rooted. His eyes were those of a much older man, serious, steady, aware.

Georgette's trance-like state popped like a soap bubble. Wrenching her wrist from the leader's grasp, she stumbled away, lifted her skirts, and ran through the woods, back to the safety of little children singing hymns around the fire. Her face burned as with fever, and she couldn't stop trembling.

In the forest, Stephen cursed violently, took a step closer to Robert, and raised his clenched fists, his face contorted. But Robert stood perfectly still, his eyes coldly contemptuous under his hood.

Stephen dropped his hands, spat on the ground and stomped away into the woods. If he had glanced behind him, he would have seen Robert drop weakly to his knees in the forest, place his palms together and bend his head in grateful prayer.

He removed his blanket and pack from the circle around Stephen and returned to his old group.

Georgette slept little that night, and when she did, she had nightmare after nightmare. The only fragment she could remember the next morning made her shudder. She was kneeling in the little church in her village and, when she raised her eyes to the beloved statue of Mother Mary in her blue gown, the hair that emerged from beneath the Madonna's head covering suddenly seemed to move, as if in a breeze, and looking more closely, she thought she saw tiny little serpents hiding among the locks, unseen by the good Mother.

That day, and the ones after, Georgette's spirits were heavy. The religious songs sounded like questions in her ears; the bread donated by enthusiastic villagers who heard the preaching of Prophet Stephen stuck in her throat. She took great care not to venture near the leader, staying near the back of the procession. And she avoided Patrice, shuddering at the thought of the girl's rough worldliness about such matters. But she did try to thank the Abbé. Twice she saw him and walked in his direction, but he seemed to melt away into the crowd. Eventually, she understood that he was reluctant to talk with her and she left him alone.

She longed for the old prickly reassuring presence of Gregor, and sometimes spoke to him in her mind, telling him of the questions that tormented her, in a way she could never have done when he was alive. The terrible encounter in the forest was something she could not bring her mind close enough to think about.

From the beginning, there had been a worm of discomfort that occasionally made her uneasy. Now it gnawed at her constantly. Had she left home for Jesus or for her own glory? Was she guilty of abandoning her father and her beloved old priest, proclaiming in her vanity a higher purpose for her little life?

And was Gregor's death only the beginning of her punishment?

CHAPTER TWELVE

Georgette noticed, without really seeing, tall buildings and crowds of people in a town called Limoges. Her perception was disoriented, as if she had been spun in a circle until she no longer knew who or where she was. Her lips moved constantly as she prayed the same Latin prayers over and over again.

Limoges marked the point at which the trees began to thin out and, for the first time, hot weather became a problem. The travellers felt as if they had emerged from a darkness to which they had grown accustomed into a bright light that burned their eyes. This southern part of France was different from any landscape they had seen before. The soil was so crumbly that they saw men working it alone without the help of neighbours or animals. But the dryness of the soil meant that the crops were thinly planted over large areas, and the land spread hot and wide between neighbours.

Now there was no easy source of meat as in the forests, and even though the boys caught many fish in the Vienne river as they followed its banks, the flesh of salmon and carp did not fill the belly as good fatty meat did. The procession moved much more slowly in the heat. This summer was particularly warm, with a continuing drought, so the harvest was poor. Long lines of grapevines bore drooping yellow little leaves and brittle tendrils. The people they passed wanted to be hospitable, offering them as much bread and milk as they could spare, but there was no single source of food big enough to feed so many bellies. The goats and sheep in this region were thin. The cows gave milk that was watery and less fatty and satisfying than the milk the northerners had grown up on; they called it blue milk.

The food that seemed to be most plentiful was olives. Outside one town, the Crusaders were offered crusty hunks of unfamiliar southern bread, made from a grain called rye, and urged to dip them in a rich, aromatic and glowing oil made from olives. Obeying listlessly, Georgette took a bite.

'Mother Mary! Your blessings never cease!' she exclaimed with her mouth still full. The group of girls sitting with her on the outskirts of the town were dipping and eating, dipping and eating, too greedily to agree with her. It was the first time she had enjoyed food, or anything else, since the forest encounter with Stephen.

The twisted olive trees with their dusty leaves grew on every hillside, even when there was no sign of water and the soil was cracked and parched. The Crusaders grew used to eating marinated olives, rye bread with olive oil, and more olives. They washed down the crusty bread with cider, while the older boys quaffed grain beer around their fires at night and laughed loudly.

They arrived in the south just as the last cherries clung to their twigs and peaches were beginning to darken in colour. Craving the fruit, many of the children made themselves sick by eating peaches that were not ripe, and stomach pains made the little ones cry at night.

Impatient to reach Marseilles, the Prophet chose what he had been told was the shortest route, leading the sun-drained group directly into the rocky Cévennes range. By the time they were halfway up a high mountain pass, it was too late to turn back. They had no breath to sing songs, nor even to speak, as they plodded up the steep path. The sun reflected off the white rocks and burned into their eyes.

'Stop whining. I'll carry you,' Georgette heard one of the older boys, Alain, say to his younger brother. Little Jean Paul was only seven and could barely reach up to the rocks they were climbing. How could Alain manage to carry Jean Paul when she, Georgette, could barely carry herself?

Of all the days of walking, this was the most strenuous. Or perhaps her mind was not as strong as it had been before that night in the forest.

The path became narrower and more precarious, and the sheer drop more and more frightening. The Crusaders pressed themselves against the cliffs, many of them holding hands tightly. Suddenly, there was a terrible, eerie scream, and Georgette looked up to see a bigger girl and a small child falling into the canyon below. They seemed to wheel around and around, and their skirts caught the air and billowed as if they were dancing in the air. They plummeted down to the riverbed far below, slamming into the ground like rag dolls. The haunting scream still rang in the air. Other children began shrieking too, their screams echoing through the mountains.

Georgette blocked her ears but she could not block her eyes from seeing the tiny crumpled bodies at the foot of the cliff. She tried to pray, but all that came out was, 'Please help us, please help us, please help us . . .'

'Everything will be all right. I'm right here. Nothing is going to happen to you,' whispered a steady, reassuring voice next to her.

Georgette opened her eyes. It was Alain, talking to his little brother. The child stood trembling violently.

He pulled his brother's shirt so strongly that Alain had to go down on his knees on the narrow stony path. Sheltered in strong, encircling arms, his brother's voice soft in his ear, the boy grew calmer. They sat down very carefully, Alain's bare knees showing the imprint of the stones he had knelt on.

Alain looked up at Georgette. 'I cannot see anything from here. Is anything happening up ahead?'

'There is nothing,' Georgette said. 'As far up the mountain as I can see, the line is stopped. No one is walking on.'

He bowed his head over the boy's head. Gradually, Georgette's heartbeat slowed and her legs stopped trembling. Slowly, she also lowered herself to the ground, sitting cross-legged just ahead of them.

'My legs feel weak,' she said to Alain, as if apologising. He did not reply but kept his lips to his little brother's head; sometimes he whispered a few words. They waited for a long time.

Eventually, instructions from the Prophet reached those near the back of the line. Apparently, the older girl had been carrying the younger when she overbalanced and fell. So they were no longer allowed to carry the little Crusaders, only to hold their hands. They had to continue climbing. There was a mountain village up ahead where they would rest.

Georgette helped Alain lift Jean Paul up giant-sized rock stairs and across narrow fissures in the dry earth. The sheer drop seemed to beckon them wickedly. The hours stretched on.

It was growing dark as they stumbled into the village of Malaucène, and after a sparse meal donated by the poor villagers, the Crusaders fell asleep without the usual boisterousness and teasing.

Georgette woke early. There were children crying, not just a few, but ten or twenty or more. She hurried to help. But many of the crying children had siblings already trying to comfort them, with no success, partly because the older siblings were crying themselves.

'What is happening?' Georgette asked Patrice, who was hugging two of the little ones, with another clinging to her skirt.

The girl whirled to face Georgette.

'Your precious prophet has ordered that all the children younger than ten years be left behind in this village.' Her eyes were red and her cheeks flushed.

'We're leaving the little ones here? But they're so far from home. How will they get back to their parents?'

'Perhaps they'll fly through the skies like we will walk through the sea at Marseilles. Oh, don't look so shocked, Georgette. Yes, that was blasphemous. And this cruel order warrants it.'

Giving the children one last tight squeeze, she strode off, with her hands cupped over her ears to block out their wails.

A short time before, Georgette would have tried to defend Stephen's decision by saying God must have ordered him to give this command for some Divine reason. Now she was silent.

It was time to travel on. Patrice had not waited for the command or for final goodbyes but walked ahead alone. Alain stood watching from the side of the road, Jean Paul's hand in his own. He and a number of other older siblings had decided to stay in this village with their little sisters or brothers, to try to find work or make their way home.

But most obeyed the Prophet's order that they should march on for the glory of Christ. The small children who were left behind screamed. Georgette bit her lip until it bled. The faces of the little children looked old and stricken, like her father's face when she left him to follow the Prophet.

The Crusaders began marching. Someone shouted back to the group of children, 'I swear by God I will return to you, Tom. Jesus Christ will lead me back. Pray to him.'

The Prophet led them onward.

CHAPTER THIRTEEN

Only anticipation of the future kept the Crusaders moving now. At night, they roused their spirits with descriptions of how the sea would part for them, as they walked across the seabed to Jerusalem. From the encouraging answers of farmers along the way, the Mediterranean Sea was not very far at all.

The travellers tried to walk more quickly. They rose very early in the morning and later, in the heat of the day, they lay for an hour or two in the shade of olive trees, as they saw the locals doing. New recruits joined them, some as young as those left behind in Malaucène. Stephen himself was presented with a horse-drawn cart by a wealthy farmer along the way, and he now travelled under a canopy that sheltered him from the sun.

Finally, one morning there was a shout from the front that travelled rapidly from group to group.

'The sea!'

Georgette strained her eyes to see what lay in the distance. On the horizon there was indeed a haze of blue.

'They said we would arrive at the sea,' she murmured. Of many things that had turned out to be not as they should, at least one thing they had been told was true.

Children shouted in excitement. Willow whistles shrieked, drums rolled and horns sounded. Triumphant songs were screamed rather than sung, each person singing the words at a different speed. Patrice rushed up to hug Georgette and then ran back into the raucous crowd.

Amid the loud and uninhibited rejoicing, there were a number of Crusaders, singly or in small groups, praying in gratitude. Georgette thanked Mother Mary, who knew the beauty of blue and had led her to the sea.

Stephen had galloped ahead with his attendants to see the sea from closer up, leaving the camp in the hands of the older boys, but those caretakers were as giddy as the small children. A spontaneous mummery of jousting, with long sticks for javelins, ended with a fistfight when one contestant was knocked to the ground. Some of the boys boldly rushed up to the girls and stole quick fondles.

For over an hour, chaos ruled. Small children were sobbing at the roughhousing. A large group of girls had gathered together like hens in the middle of a fox-besieged enclosure. Under Patrice's energetic leadership, they linked arms and shouted at the boys not to dare take advantage of them. Some of them swore. The boys swore back, much more crudely.

Then Prophet Stephen returned, positioning himself atop a high rock. The unruly Crusaders gradually became aware of his still presence. They grew quiet, with only the echoes of shouts dissolving in the air. Prophet Stephen's eyes were glazed over. He lifted his arms high. Georgette remembered the puppet show that some travellers had once brought to her village. Stephen was the puppet and God was the puppeteer. Or perhaps Stephen was the puppeteer and the Crusaders his puppets.

He began to preach. 'Behold, ye Crusaders, how Jesus Christ has led us to the sea, exactly as he promised when he visited me as I sat with my sheep. Is this not a joyous day?'

His voice hummed eerily in the dry, clear air and the listeners swayed as if hypnotised. But Georgette averted her eyes. She could not think clearly about what had happened, and what could have happened further, in the dark forest that night. She wished she could thrill to the Prophet's words as the others were doing.

'Tomorrow we will reach Marseilles and we will march in formation to the harbour. For God Himself is preparing the path for us. God Himself will hold apart the sea for us. Yea, the Miracle approaches. For the Lord promised me in my dream that the seas would part for children to walk across on dry water to the Promised Land. He summoned me as he summoned our prophet Moses, to lead the chosen, the beloved ones, the pure of heart, to free Jerusalem from the infidels. There we will raise high the banner of Christ in its rightful place.'

Suddenly, Georgette imagined the banner of Christ flying in the breeze that Jesus once felt, fluttering above the earth he once walked. Her soul thrilled. Truly, whatever the faults of man, God was great, and she bowed her head willingly in her love for Him, the Perfect One.

They marched into the city of Marseilles in the late afternoon of the following day. They could have arrived much earlier, but in the morning Stephen had called the Crusaders together in a grand assembly, to be their last in France.

To set the scene, a hastily rehearsed theatrical tableau of the hymn *Ave Maris Stella* was presented, with a very pretty girl dressed as Mother Mary, Star of the Sea. After the crowd's enthusiastic applause, Stephen majestically summoned the group leaders, each one bedecked with an item of finery bestowed on the Prophet by admirers along the way. Some proud, some embarrassed, each stepped forward in turn and was blessed by the Prophet. The most articulate of them, having learned some sleight of tongue from Stephen, presented a tribute to the great

Prophet, who had inspired this glorious mission and kept them safe. Finally, Stephen, by far the most resplendent of all, thanked the leaders for their service to God and blessed the youngest child among them, as a symbol of the innocent and pure love that permeated their Crusade.

The carefully choreographed ceremony made Georgette uneasy. *What about Gregor and the many hundreds or even thousands of others who died or were abandoned along the way*, she wanted to ask. *Why are our losses not mentioned, only our triumph? It has not been a golden journey, sometimes it was black and frightening. That too should be remembered.* And, anyway, they had not yet reached their goal, so why were they congratulating their leaders here in France? Why not at the true end of the pilgrimage, in Jerusalem?

By the time they reached the gates of Marseilles, word of their approach had spread and townspeople lined the streets, cheering and marvelling at the palpable energy of these young people who had travelled such a long way. Some knelt when Prophet Stephen's cart passed, the canopy removed so that he could be seen in his splendour, bearing aloft the gold crucifix. Women pressed bread and fruit into the children's hands, calling them little prophets and asking for blessings, but the Crusaders were too buoyed by excitement to feel hungry.

CHAPTER FOURTEEN

At the first light of dawn, the Crusaders picked themselves up from wherever they had snatched a restless sleep, on the cobblestone pavements of Marseilles, in a garden, before the hearths of kindly families.

Stephen had made a brief speech the previous night, sitting astride a fresh horse without dismounting, his eyes blinking fearfully as he searched for words. When he had preached in the past, inspiration had raised him from the earth of ordinary humans like a soaring kite. He had been enraptured, transformed by his vision. Now his words were but those of the uneducated shepherd that he truly was. His face was stricken and white; his hands trembled. *He is genuinely shocked*, Robert realised. *He really thought the waters would part, just as Christ – or perhaps a dark spirit masquerading as Christ – had promised him.*

'Children. Crusaders. I think – I think God doesn't want us to walk on the sea – through the sea – in the dark and it is close to dark now. In the morning the waters will separate, will part. And we will get to the Holy Land. So come back here in the morning and you will surely see a miracle.' He had looked out over the crowd and opened his mouth to say more, but seemed to lose courage. He had wheeled his horse around and disappeared into the maze of alleyways like a fox just ahead of the hounds.

Now it was morning. Patrice held Georgette's hand comfortingly as they returned to the quay. The younger children ran eagerly, but the others walked slowly and with dread. At the sight of the sea – still unchanged, still impassable – they all stood still. There was nowhere to go.

Suddenly, a girl ran on to the quay, her voice wild and angry. 'He's stolen my sister! Prophet Stephen has stolen my beautiful sister!'

The others gazed at her uncomprehendingly.

'He came to get her when we lay down to sleep. He took her away with him!' the girl shouted, her face blotchy with rage. 'He said her sweet voice could inspire his group through the night. But when I woke up this morning, I saw that she hadn't returned. I ran to Stephen's guard, but he said no one sang to them last night. Stephen hasn't been seen at all.'

She sobbed bitterly, her pitch rising, and all heard her clearly in the still dawn air. 'His white charger is gone too. He has ridden off with my sister. Oh, the treachery! How we trusted and followed him.'

To a child who dared to shout a disbelieving 'No!', she turned fiercely and screamed, 'He will not lead us to the Promised Land. His promise was a lie. And he has disappeared!'

Another girl shouted out, 'My brother died for this?'

Georgette recognised her as the twin whose frail spindly brother was the first to succumb to fever when they were camping in the Count of Gallardon's meadow.

'He died so that we could reach Jerusalem, not Marseilles!'

There were cries of agreement. Crusaders milled aimlessly around the wet, dirty wharf. Slowly, it began to dawn on the youngsters that they had nowhere to go. They had become accustomed to orders and directions, and there had been a clear and common goal. Now it had disappeared, and they were far from home and alone.

'What will we do now?' a little boy sobbed.

The road home would be much harder even than their journey to Marseilles. Winter would soon be upon them and, as bad as the heat had been, particularly during the last part of their journey, the cold would be many times worse. Villagers would not feel inspired to offer food to those returning from a failed Crusade. Crops had been poor because of the hot summer and the ongoing drought, and many farming families were hungry themselves.

'I will look for work here in Marseilles,' Patrice told Georgette. 'Will you stay too?'

Georgette shook her head. Patrice had seven brothers and sisters at home. But Georgette was now an only child. She had a duty to return home, to look after her father and Father David. And she had the terrible obligation to tell her father of his only son's death.

The noise on the wharf was becoming louder and more intense. Some of the Crusaders were angry. Some were frightened. There was no centre to hold them together. Several of them began to batter, first with words and then with their fists, an older boy who had been one of the Prophet's inner circle. Perceiving that the winds of fortune had changed, several other former lieutenants slipped away from the harbour. Younger children hurried after them, trailed back to the quayside, then scampered off again, like lambs uncertain which leader to follow.

One girl suggested that the waters might part on the next day, or the one after that, if they were all patient and kept their faith. Patrice grimaced. She was ready to follow those who had already departed to try to find work ahead of the crowd. But the smallest children called out their agreement that there was still hope, then plopped down on the dirty wharf with their little bundles, exhausted, glad for the rest, and certain that someone, or God, would take care of them.

It was at this time of confusion that their attention was drawn by two large men standing above the crowd on a raised part of the wharf.

'Young people!' one of them bellowed, a seafaring man from the looks of his wide pants and jacket, neither of which were very clean. 'Children of God,' he shouted several times, until all the children turned towards him. His face was marbled with scars from smallpox and his chin jutted out belligerently.

'I am Hugh Ferreus, called Hugh the Iron. I welcome you to our city of Marseilles. It is commendable that you have travelled so far in your great and pure love for Christ. I too love our Lord and wish to serve Him. Thus I am offering you free passage to the Holy Land. I am the owner of seven merchant ships that are due to leave France shortly for my trading post in the port of Akko, close to Jerusalem. I cannot do miracles like your young leader. And him not too well either, it seems. The seas will not part for you. But with the kind sponsorship of William of Posquières, called William the Pig, next to me, you may travel to the Holy Land the way of mere mortals, by sail.'

He gestured to his companion, who was clearly a man of some wealth but no noble blood, a merchant surely. The merchant waved a plump white hand in the air, acknowledging the introduction with a self-satisfied smile on his fleshy lips. Indeed, he looked much like a pig.

Hugh the Iron continued, 'The captains of the seven ships will be ordered to ready their ships immediately in order to transport you across the seas to your destination.'

'Praise be to God,' William the Pig added in a high-pitched voice.

Patrice gave a little bounce at Georgette's side. The Crusaders burst into exclamations but quickly quieted when Hugh the Iron waved his hands for order.

'We cannot fit all of you on to the ships. We will try to carry as many of you as possible. If you are willing to eschew some comfort on your holy journey, I will be able to offer passage to a greater number.'

'I must prepare my ships for this unexpected opportunity to serve God. Stay here at the quay if you wish to take this God-given chance. When we are ready, you may be among the lucky chosen children.' Hugh the Iron strode from the harbour and William the Pig waddled off behind him.

There was chaos. Each one longed fiercely to be chosen ahead of someone else. The atmosphere had changed to one of competition and rivalry. They squabbled over space to sit or lie on the long, narrow quay.

Georgette was torn. She wanted to reach the Holy Land, even though the pilgrimage had been, so far, a journey of confusion, loss and fear. And this was surely a practical alternative to walking across the bed of the ocean. But when the captain was calling his offer a God-given opportunity, she had had the distinct, desolate sense that the presence of God was withdrawing.

Surely God will rejoin us at the other side of the sea, she told herself. But it seemed a long time to wait.

Patrice was in excellent spirits, chattering about going on a ship for the first time, travelling to foreign climes. The Crusaders ate, slept and defecated on the wharf, unwilling to leave for a more comfortable resting spot, in case they missed their chance to be chosen to go to Jerusalem.

Their fourth day on the wharf was unseasonably hot from early in the morning. As the youngsters sprawled listlessly without shade or shelter, the two men marched back on to the quay with purposeful tread.

'The ships are ready to sail,' Hugh the Iron boomed from his raised position, pointing to seven large ships that had been moved closer to the quay the previous day. 'Those who wish to take up our offer should form a line along the edge of the quay, and the good merchant William and I will make our selection.'

Boys and girls raced to be near the front, pushing and shoving. A number of young ones were knocked to the ground by the stampede, and stood up weeping but nevertheless hurrying to secure a place. Patrice was agile and fast, and made it to the first hundred. Georgette was strangely reluctant to hurry, and stepped into line near the back.

The sun beat down, and the water and mead provided to them by well-wishers was not sufficient. But few risked leaving the wharf to search for more. Some swayed where they stood.

After some time, Georgette slipped up to the men moving slowly down the line, motioning certain Crusaders to proceed to the gangplanks of the seven ships, waving the others away dismissively.

'Kind sirs,' she said, 'is there water for us? We are all thirsty, but the youngest children suffer the most.'

Brusquely, barely looking at her, Hugh the Iron jerked his thumb towards the open square beyond the wharf.

'There's a well at the far end of that plaza. But mind you don't disturb the line now. Those who give up their place might lose their chance to be selected.'

Georgette would lose little by giving up her place near the back and going to drink while she could. She urged the smallest children to join her. Who knew if the ships would have enough water aboard for them to drink their fill? Some were too tired to join her but others trailed along to the well. A number of the older ones stepped out of the line and followed.

Georgette and the older ones pulled up bucket after bucket until their shoulders ached. Georgette bade each person carry water in his or her clay mug or wooden bowl back to those still in the line.

'Be careful not to spill,' she warned. 'And give first to the youngest.'

When the mugs of cool water appeared, more Crusaders broke from the line and hurried to the plaza. Ragged gaps opened. Hugh the Iron glared at Georgette as she walked past him to take her place again.

The sun had passed its midpoint by the time the men neared the back of the line. William the Pig was scrawling a stroke on a grubby piece of parchment to represent each child allowed on to the boats. As he reached Georgette, he stopped and wiped the sweat from his face with a dirty cloth. Then he laboriously counted up the strokes, crossing out each group when he reached one hundred.

'Up to seven hundred now,' he told Hugh the Iron. 'That's a hundred in each boat. If we squeeze them, we can fit another twenty-five on each boat, I'm sure.'

They turned to face the line of children again and the seaman scowled at Georgette.

'You're the water-fetcher,' he sneered.

Georgette was silent.

'Any older brothers or cousins with you?'

'Not any more,' Georgette answered. 'I mean . . . no, sir.'

With a wave of dismissal, Hugh the Iron said, 'No room for troublemakers on the boat.'

And he turned to the next in line.

Robert had known from the early days, perhaps alone among all the Crusaders, that Prophet Stephen was a fake and a charlatan. Robert had never believed the seas would part for them, never believed they would finally reach Jerusalem. How dare the boy promise a miracle? The only miracle was that he had induced them all, yes, even Robert himself, to follow him. A liar and an actor, with the gift of persuasion as his dangerous weapon.

But Robert felt no pleasure at the accuracy of his assessments. He ground his teeth and pumped his fist repeatedly into his other hand in fury at Stephen's cowardly flight. The Crusaders were lost and in anguish, their faith at risk, their questions unanswered. And he, Robert, was too shy, too fearful of rebuff, to try to help.

But then the two swaggering men appeared and conveniently offered free passage to Jerusalem. Their ships were impressive, equipped with the new sternpost rudders that a traveller had described shortly before Robert left the abbey at Blois. Even though he did not like the look of the merchant and the seaman at all, this was, for the very first time, a realistic opportunity, a credible chance to reach the Holy Land.

Was it really possible that he would be able to see Jerusalem? He had so many painful questions about the Crusades, and the persecution along the way. Maybe they would be answered there in the birthplace of Jesus. He lined up with alacrity and declined to go to the well, in case he lost his place.

'How old are you?' Hugh the Iron asked when the boy's turn came.

'Fifteen,' Robert answered, looking the man straight in the eye. He had heard several lying about their age but he would never stoop to lie in order to enter the land of God. That would be soiling the purity of the pilgrimage.

William the Pig brought his quill to the parchment to draw a mark, but Hugh put out a hand to stop him and whispered something in his companion's ear. The merchant peered shortsightedly into Robert's face and Robert looked directly back. There was a hesitation. Then Hugh the Iron waved his arm to dismiss the boy and moved on to the next person in line.

Robert stood still. Had he imagined it or had he been passed over? Why didn't the men wave him towards the ships? Hugh the Iron glanced back and saw him still waiting. 'Move along, boy,' he growled. 'You're in our way.' There was no doubt.

Stunned, his mind whirling, Robert stepped away from the water and leaned against a wall.

It was not long before the men selected their last passenger, dismissed those still waiting hopefully in line, and signalled for the gangplanks to be raised. The crews on each ship must have been prepared to leave at a moment's notice. As soon as the anchors were lifted and the mooring ropes untied, lines of rowers plied their oars so that the seven vessels slipped out of the harbour with surprising speed. Within ten minutes, the young passengers were out of sight. Hugh the Iron and William the Pig strode from the wharf.

It was over.

PART THREE

A Very Different Journey

CHAPTER FIFTEEN

Georgette waved her kerchief in the air wildly, long after Patrice and the others on the boats could possibly have discerned her on the wharf. But in her imagination, she could still see the lucky chosen ones singing lustily and excitedly on the rocking deck. She pictured Patrice, glorying in another adventure, and smiled. The boats followed each other in a line, a chain, and she felt connected with them until the last one was just a speck. Then the chain snapped. She was not part of the Children's Crusade any longer. She would never reach the Promised Land.

Instead, she was one of many hundreds of children standing without purpose or direction on the quayside. Suddenly, she missed Gregor fiercely. The others did not come from her village, would not know the way home, even if they wanted to help. And they were all preoccupied with their own worries. What was she to do now, alone in this big city? She could never make the long trip home without her brother, without the crowds of singing Crusaders, without the generous gifts of food and lodging provided by pious villagers along the way. Georgette slumped to the ground and sobbed.

All for naught, all for naught. Robert's adventure was over, with nothing to show for it, except churning questions about faith and the evil of man. Robert's legs were aching, yet he would not sit down. That would be admitting that it was all for naught. The false prophet had deluded his flock and deserted them, but no earthly punishment would befall him. Only after his death would he be called to account. And now Robert was alone in a strange city, far from the abbey, his only home, where he felt he no longer belonged.

No, not alone. Robert's eyes widened as he saw a young girl waving a white cloth frantically at the departing boats. It was the girl who had revived his wilting faith with her perfect devotion to God when her brother took sick and died. It was the girl he could not bear to see violated by Stephen's lust; the one he had dared to save. She too had been rejected. She too was alone in Marseilles. No, not alone.

He watched as Georgette sat on the wharf and wept, longing to comfort her but hesitant. The new confidence he had felt as a leading member of the Crusade had fled and he was consumed with shyness. He took a deep breath, picked up his little sack and walked close to Georgette, sitting down silently behind her until she finished with her tears.

When Georgette's sobs quieted, she dried her swollen eyes with her apron. Most of the crowd had disappeared, gone she knew not where. The youngsters clustering in a few small groups around the harbour seemed as lost as she did, and none of them were familiar to her. Should she try to attach herself to one of the groups? She could not take the risk of being left alone on the road if the group split in different directions once they reached central France. What if the older boys thought they could take liberties with her in her distress and helplessness?

She felt, rather than saw, the presence of someone directly behind her. She whirled around quickly and relaxed with a little sigh. It was the boy they called the Abbé.

He approached. Bending a little, he said, 'Good eve, mistress. May I sit beside you?'

She wanted to giggle at the formality: was she a fine lady sitting on a velvet bench that he should talk so? But his politeness and respect were so sincere, without affectation or falsity, that she couldn't hurt his feelings.

'Yes, if you please,' she responded.

'Your name is Georgette,' he stated and she looked at him with surprise. 'I am Robert, of the Abbey of Blois,' he offered. They sat side by side for a while. She stole a glance at his face below the hood and saw that he too was sombre and disappointed.

'It feels hard not to be chosen,' she ventured, and he nodded. For a long time they remained still on the dirty quayside.

As dusk deepened, Georgette noticed that they were the only young people still on the wharf. Two drunken sailors swaggered past without seeing them in the shadows, and one stopped, faced a wall close to them, and pulled at his trousers. Georgette had time only to jerk her skirts away from the piss whooshing against the stones so near to her. Robert caught her arm, lifted her to her feet and guided her away from the harbour.

'I saw a few taverns on the way through the town,' he said. 'Perhaps we can find somewhere to sleep for the night and some hot food.'

Georgette blinked. *We?* He was talking as though they had already decided to throw in their fates together. She opened her mouth to protest her ignorance of such an agreement, but closed it. There was great relief in having this quiet older boy at her side and she would not disturb his assumption until she had another and better solution.

Too drained and shy to talk, they entered the first inn silently and waited to be noticed. The innkeeper took one look at their youthful faces and apparent lack of funds and told them roughly to be off: the inn was full and he would not tolerate beggars. Georgette blushed and quickly lifted the hem of her cape, about to dig for the bits of silver sewn in there when her father had urged them on her. Quickly, Robert put his hand on her arm again, with that respectful but firm grasp, and led her out of the door.

'Do not reveal that you have a hiding place for coins,' he warned. 'Take them out here, in this alley, where no one will see.' And he began to pick with a little knife at something stitched behind his own belt, which turned out to be a cloth knotted around coins. Georgette borrowed his knife and undid her own even little stitches, trustingly dropped her coins into the same pile as his, and counted the total along with him. At the next inn they entered, Robert showed a little of their money in his hand as he asked for lodging, and the innkeeper seemed regretful as he said he had more guests than straw pallets and could not even squeeze them into a room with other customers. He directed them to the third, and last, inn in the area of the harbour.

Outside the entrance, Georgette whispered, 'What will we do if they too are full?'

Robert did not answer but appeared determined as he opened the thick door. They were met by the warmth and delicious smell of a huge fire licking eagerly at several chickens and a fatty lamb shank on a large spit. The juices dripped and sizzled on the willow-wood below. The woman turning the spit handed over her task to a sturdy child, mopped her brow and came towards them, her expression surprised but not unfriendly at the sight of two young, unaccompanied guests. She looked keenly at Robert as he requested shelter and food, counted the coins in his hand, and clucked at the sight of Georgette's swollen, red eyes.

'I have no rooms,' she began, at which Georgette's face must have fallen because the woman continued hurriedly, 'but don't ye worry, there is room enough for ye to lay down near the fire tonight after my good dinner. Ye will be warm there and if ye don't mind the noise of those who might stay up late drinking, ye'll sleep well and feel brighter in the morning.'

She took some of the silver from Robert's palm, closed his fingers around the other coins and bade him tuck them away safely, and led them to the broad slabs of stone before the fire, which she promised to soften with straw before they went to bed.

The aromatic lamb shank turned out to be for the sole pleasure of two well-dressed men who entered in high spirits after all the other guests had dined on chicken. With many compliments, the innkeeper ushered these particular guests into a private alcove, warmed by its own small fire and shielded from curious eyes by a greasy curtain. The new arrivals did not notice the young boy and girl sitting on the hearthstones, but Robert and Georgette recognised the seafaring man and the merchant from the quayside. Hugh the Iron and William the Pig.

Robert's face reddened; Georgette's lips trembled. They needed no reminder of the failure of the day.

All the other guests had retired to bed by this time, and while the innkeeper fawned over the two men, Robert and Georgette settled down silently before the fire. The hearth was so long that they could lie with the top of their heads pointing towards each other. The woman had provided a good amount of straw, and they both felt the dying embers warming them all the way along to their toes. Georgette yawned and heard Robert respond in kind.

But the men in the alcove were becoming increasingly quarrelsome as they quaffed their beer, and soon their angry voices became loud enough to be clearly overheard.

'I'll not take that loss all on myself. I had my timber ready at the dock on time and paid good money to have it loaded on your ships. I paid more good money to have it unloaded to make room for those brats. Now what am I to do with my timber? It will be weeks until I can hire so many ships at one time again.'

'Damn your timber, man,' Hugh the Iron roared, his rough voice cutting across the merchant's whine. 'We'll get triple the profit from the new cargo, maybe more.'

'Yes, we both profit, but 'tis my money that is financing this voyage, including all the food I had to provide for those ragamuffins,' William the Pig complained. 'You know yourself that we picked the sturdiest, and those kind eat more, don't they?'

'And sell for more too.'

The merchant merely grunted in response, so Hugh pressed his advantage.

'Anyway, the way they're squeezed on, I'm taking a greater risk of my boats being sunk before we can hand over the goods. Enough about your timber, merchant William, and pay the money you owe me.'

William the Pig let loose a flood of oaths, but pushed back his chair in defeat.

'Upstairs,' he said. 'We can count it out in private there.'

Georgette was pressing her knuckles against her mouth to keep from screaming. Robert felt a rage so violent and painful that a groan escaped him. But the men stumbling from the room were far too drunk to notice.

Silence.

There could be no doubt. The men who claimed they were offering free passage as a service to God expected to make a profit on each child. The Crusaders who had marched singing on to those seven boats, the ones Georgette had thought so fortunate to be chosen, were going to be sold like pieces of timber.

Recollecting the scene on the wharf in a flash, Georgette realised that her interference on behalf of the thirsty children had made her seem too independent to be chosen. But Robert? He was tall, if not sturdy. Was there something in his straight, unblinking gaze that had unnerved them?

When Georgette and Robert heard the men's feet creaking overhead, they sat up slowly. Robert was silent, his face red and blotchy. Georgette sobbed like a lost child.

After a few minutes, Robert put his arm around her shoulders, awkward but comforting. She barely realised that she was gripping his jerkin and weeping into his shoulder, stifling the noise against the cloth. She had cried bitterly twice that day, once because she had not been on the ship, and the second time because she could have been on the ship . . . and because Patrice and so many others just like her were sailing in their innocence to a terrible fate.

'Can't we save them?' she cried. 'Is there no one who can save them?'

Robert's currency was thoughts, not feelings. He began to speak his thoughts out loud. And she quietened and listened.

'They will be far away by now. Any pursuit by good men here in Marseilles, if there be good men any longer, will fail to catch up with those ships. So there is no way to reach them and free them.' At this, he shuddered, still holding Georgette around her shoulders protectively.

He continued, 'We know some of the children's names and we can retrace our route, in order to tell the parents of their sad fate.'

Georgette lifted her face. 'But perhaps it is better for them not to know; to think their children are in the Holy Land, or even that they are dead and at peace,' she whispered.

'You know more about these things than I do,' Robert said.

'What about the innkeeper?' Georgette said. 'She was kind. Is there no one we can tell?'

'Aye, we can tell a priest of this town what we heard,' Robert replied. 'So that Hugh and William are put on trial for their terrible work. The Holy Roman Emperor himself must blanch at the evil in men who could trade in child pilgrims. But the men will vehemently deny any knowledge of the plot, and it will be our word, two young northerners, against the word of two rich traders from this big southern city.'

There was a long silence while they traced each of their options to a dead end. Then Robert spoke with difficulty,

'We must bear the truth alone for now. And thank God, for saving us from being among the chosen ones.'

The youngsters reeled with shock and sheer exhaustion. Georgette swayed as she sat and Robert urged her to try to sleep.

'This is no place for young people without protectors,' he said. 'Tomorrow, if you are agreeable, we should start back to the north.'

Georgette nodded. She was grateful for the company. But when she closed her eyes, she saw the merry children waving from the deck of the last boat and she began to sob again. Robert stretched out his arm and took one of her hands. And that was how they slept, each with an arm outstretched to the other.

CHAPTER SIXTEEN

As soon as they left town the next day, returning heavily along the same road the Crusaders had fair danced along only a week before, Georgette felt the change in the weather. A cool wind swirled leaves off the trees and into circles of dust. Sometimes when Georgette woke, wound tightly in her blankets, she found herself lying close to Robert for warmth. Shy, she moved away quietly before he awoke.

They tried to spend their coins sparingly on food along the way, but Robert insisted that they eat at least once every day and drink frequently from the streams they passed.

'We need our strength,' he stated, in that way he had of speaking as though they were a single unit.

When all but one small coin of their money had run out, they swallowed their pride and begged for food. Mostly they were met with rejection or food destined for the pig trough. Sometimes they were treated kindly and given enough food that they could divide it into several small meals for the journey. For a few weeks, they supplemented their meagre diet with the last pears left on the trees and little wild apples, sour and twisted and delicious. They picked more than they could eat, and Georgette filled the pockets of her apron.

Along the way they talked or were silent. Robert loved to hear her stories about Father David, about his gentleness, humility and wisdom. His own relationship with his mentor had, he now realised, none of the inspiration and moral guidance that Georgette had experienced.

'I pray that I will meet your Father David in person,' he said one day. 'I talk sometimes to my own teacher in my head, asking him the questions that tormented me on our journey with the Crusaders, but I cannot anticipate that his answers will satisfy my spirit. From what you tell of him, I believe Father David would be able to separate the twisted strands of my thoughts and bring me some clarity and peace.'

'Indeed he will help you,' Georgette answered with absolute confidence.

'His influence glows within you, Georgette,' Robert replied. 'You were the first girl I was ever drawn to. When you prayed next to –' He hesitated, but Georgette's eyes did not falter. '. . . your brother at his death, you renewed something in me that I thought was gone.'

Georgette flushed and they continued on their way. When the road was rough, he took her hand to help her, and kept it for a long time.

On one glorious day, with the sun apparently confused as to the season, they stopped to try their luck at fishing in a pond. Within a minute or two, using Georgette's cap as a net, they scooped up a barbotte fish with surprising ease. It was rare luck, for they never caught another that way. They lit a fire with Robert's flint and fed it with the plentiful twigs on the ground.

The fish was large and fleshy and Georgette speared it carefully on a branch and smoked rather than roasted it. Patiently she turned it every few minutes, and when she was sure the inside was cooked through, she lowered it to brown the skin briefly and served it with a flourish on a large flat leaf.

'Robert, let us take a Sabbath day and rest until tomorrow morning,' she begged as they ate hungrily. Robert smiled at her for answer as they sat together on the blankets in the sun, their stomachs deliciously full, their spirits higher than they had been since leaving Marseilles.

'I see I shall never lack for well-cooked food with thee.'

Georgette trembled at his words. This was the furthest he had gone in his assumption of partnership with her. They had not yet spoken of the future after this long journey reached its close. What did he mean?

Robert's hood cast shadows on his eyes and cheek-bones. He never removed it, day or night. Georgette wanted to see his face properly, didn't want shadows and hiding and secrets between them. Taking a chance, she reached out and took the rim of the cowl in her fingers, looking questioningly at him. But he only looked down, his face suddenly sad and apprehensive and resigned, all at once. As she pushed the hood back very carefully, it fell completely away, to his shoulders, and she saw clearly the raised angry scar stretching from the outside of one eyebrow to the jawline just below his earlobe.

The boy made a quick gesture, reaching to pull the cloth back over himself again, but Georgette caught his hand and held it in one of hers. Without hesitation she traced the bumpy rope with soft, sympathetic fingers, before moving on to trace the well-formed sculpture of his head, the height of his forehead, the neat ears, all so new to her.

'You are handsome and well formed, Robert,' Georgette murmured.

Gradually, the blush of Robert's skin faded. He put out his own hand and lifted her chin so that he could look directly into her eyes. Drawing her into his arms, he lowered his lips to hers. He was not smooth and experienced, but his quiet steadiness was so different from the snatched, ill-placed and clumsy kisses she had experienced on a few occasions in the village from loutish boys.

He pulled her closer, kissing and caressing her. Her body responded and she felt as if she were falling. Her hands cradled the sides of his face, and her touch on that hidden area, which had not felt even the sun for years, seemed to inflame him. They lay back on the blanket and he kissed her neck and ears and throat, his breathing growing quicker and deeper.

They were in a storm of love together and, if he had asked, she would have given herself to him without hesitation. She felt love for him so powerful in her body and heart that it was as if, in the eyes of God, they were married. But Robert was still the Abbé and would not take what was not yet his, by the law of the Church. With a groan he dropped his hands and turned his back to her, controlling his ardour with difficulty.

She remained silent, confused, and her arms felt cold from the absence of him.

He did not turn back to face her until his breathing was fairly even again. Then he drew her to him with tenderness and kissed the top of her head. They lay there in utter happiness, watching the blue-and-white glory above them until they both fell asleep.

CHAPTER SEVENTEEN

When, by Robert's reckoning, they were about two thirds of the way to Georgette's home, they began to feel the pain of real hunger. The villagers in this area were inhospitable, grumbling that whether King Philippe Auguste declared it officially or not, they were in the midst of yet another famine year. Georgette and Robert used their last coin to buy food, but after such a dry season, the coin did not purchase as much as it would have in the spring.

They found a few old turnips in an abandoned field, which kept them going for a few days. Some of the farmers allowed them to sleep with the animals in the barn, so fortunately they were not totally exposed to the elements. It had not snowed yet, but Robert dreaded the first snowfall.

'It's not only the cold that concerns me,' he mused aloud to Georgette, in his way. 'The twigs will be wet and not easy to light. The track may be obliterated if the snow is heavy. I pray the skies will stay clear until we reach your father.'

Their luck ran out a few days later. They had not eaten for more than a day, not since a villager had given them some old bread that she had intended to feed to her pigs.

'Be off with ye now,' she ordered as she almost threw them the crusts. 'I'm too busy nursing me sick children to be disturbed by beggars.'

They thanked her politely and said they would pray for her sick children, but the door had already been slammed in their faces. The bread had lain hard but filling in their bellies as they continued on the road.

Now Robert stopped and observed the sky. 'It looks like snow,' he observed. 'We will need a barn to sleep in tonight.' But by nightfall they had met with no sign of human habitation.

Robert stopped walking and looked around him.

'We have to find shelter of any kind,' Robert said. 'I feel the first snowflakes, and besides, I am sick.'

Georgette glanced at him in panic. He did indeed look pale and there was sweat above his lips.

'You've caught the ague,' Georgette cried, as she put her cool hand on Robert's clammy and burning forehead. Perhaps it was the bread from the house where children were sick. There was no sense in thinking about how he had caught it.

'There,' Georgette exclaimed, pointing at an abandoned haystack.

'It's as good a place to spend the night as we are likely to find,' Robert conceded. They burrowed into the centre of the crackly hay and pulled it over them, leaving a narrow passage for fresh air. Through the passage they could watch the snow coming down, but soon it was too dark to see out. Their sleeping hole was not much colder than an ill-maintained barn, and it was not the first time they had slept in the rough heart of a haystack. But it was the first time one of them had been ill. Robert was restless in the night, alternately shivering and sweating, but in the morning he insisted on pressing on.

''Tis but a chill I have caught. That, and the dust in the hay. It seemed to enter my very lungs in the night.'

The snow had ceased after thinly coating the ground, but the weather echoed their mood, grey and depressed. Instead of lightening, as the noon hour approached, the sky became darker and more threatening. When they had been travelling for some hours at a slow pace, snow started to fall again. At first, Georgette barely noticed the big flakes, concentrating as she was on supporting Robert's weight without making it clear that she was doing more than clasping his elbow. In her other hand, she carried both his bundle and her own, and he did not even protest. But when the flakes on her eyelashes made it necessary for her to stop, put down the bundles, and wipe her eyes so she could see clearly, she was alarmed to notice for the first time that the snow had already fallen thick on the ground and showed no sign of ending.

'Must stay on the road,' Robert murmured. 'Mustn't get lost.'

'I cannot see the road any more,' Georgette replied, desperation in her voice.

'Then we must stop right here.' His voice was so soft she barely heard him.

Georgette obeyed because she could think of nothing else.

Robert slumped to the ground and Georgette lay down next to him, wrapping him in both blankets. She prayed for what seemed like hours, while Robert drifted in and out of sleep. She prayed mostly for him, but she prayed too for the flawed, failed, fatal Crusade.

'I wanted to suffer for You, Jesus,' she whispered. I wanted to prove that I loved You. But nothing on that pilgrimage brought glory to Your name by imitating the goodness of Jesus Christ. Nay, the opposite. Like the Crusaders who passed here before us, we showed those poor infidels an army of cruelty and force, torturing and violating. What now must they think of those who worship Christ? If only they knew Father David.'

She turned her head in the direction of her home. 'Wise old Father David, you did not want me to join this crusade. But I was in a fervour, a shallow dream, bewitched by my imagination. I was impatient and impulsive and did not wish to see that your spirit was troubled.'

Robert trembled violently and sometimes moaned with pain, pressing his hands to his temples. For a while there was only the sound of Robert's chattering teeth and laboured breathing. When the night reached its blackest hour, Robert squeezed her hand and spoke in a weak, small voice.

'Georgette, if I die here, I ask that you find my teacher and deliver a message.'

'Don't speak so,' she begged. 'In the morn we will meet with some villager who will give us shelter until you are well, and we will be on our journey home again soon. You will deliver the message yourself.'

Robert squeezed her hand again, more urgently this time. 'Not enough strength to argue. Please listen.'

Georgette deliberately composed herself. He was right, as always.

'Yes, Robert.'

'Find Abbot Benedict at the Abbey of Blois. Tell him I thank him for his care of me, for educating and guiding me. Tell him the Crusade was not as I hoped and expected . . . that violence and evil overcame compassion and devotion . . . My soul is confused. Ask him to pray for me.'

He didn't talk any more. Georgette lay down behind him and slipped one arm under his burning cheek, the other across his chest, keeping her body and legs as close to his as she could and tightening the roll of blankets like a cocoon around him. *If I can just keep him warm*, she told herself, *just keep him warm.*

CHAPTER EIGHTEEN

Georgette woke some unknown time later because someone was lifting her away from Robert. With the little strength left in her arms, she held on to Robert, muttering, 'No, no, have to keep him warm.'

'It will be better for him and for you if you will loose your hold, young one, and let me put you both into my cart,' a man's voice said, and she waked enough to see a dark shape leaning over her, silhouetted against a cold dawn sky. The Lord had heard her prayers. 'Truly, Jesus is great,' she whispered, but the man did not reply with an 'Amen'.

He had turned his attention to Robert, dragging him with difficulty to a rough cart stopped right behind them on the track. The steam from the man's heavy breathing mingled with that from an extraordinarily ugly horse chomping at the bit. The man would not be able to lift Robert into the cart, Georgette thought, her body aching to sink back into sleep. She must get up and help.

Muttering some strange words that she couldn't make out, the man desperately heaved Robert halfway up the side of the cart, and she caught up with him just in time to help raise the burden, so that the body went over the wooden ledge and dropped down on to some empty sacks and a little straw.

'Good girl,' the man said, leaning his back against the cart with a soft groan. 'Now you climb up there too and I'll take you both home to my wife. She will know what to do.'

The horse's gait was as awkward as his looks. As he stumbled along, Georgette slid from side to side with every lurch. Robert's body was limp and his eyes closed. She tried to hold him still against the jolting, but he knocked against the side of the cart again and again without any sign of consciousness. And again and again, Georgette prayed that the body she was trying to hold still was not lifeless.

The man knew Robert was past hearing and he must have thought the girl had long been asleep, for he did not lower his voice as he talked with his wife before the fire in their simple farmhouse.

'Crusaders! In our home,' the woman said.

'They're not Crusaders, they're only children,' he protested.

'What kind of parents allow their children to march off at this age, Samuel? If we had had a child . . .' Her voice cracked.

'The kind of parents who believe what the priests tell them,' was his reply.

Georgette was lying on a straw pallet close to Robert's still form, drowsy and warm but keeping herself awake to watch the precious sight of Robert's chest moving slightly, rhythmically. Each breath carried a message. *I am alive. I did not die out there in the snow. I am still with you.*

When she realised what the man and woman were saying, she almost spoke up. *It was my choice. My father and Father David did not want me to go, but they couldn't stop me.* But her fatigue, combined with her desire not to contradict the hosts who had saved their lives, overwhelmed her impulse.

The wife spoke again. 'And the danger to us? To the whole village? That boy is so weak. If anything happens to them here, you know we'll be blamed.'

The man shrugged helplessly. 'What else was there for me to do, Hannah? Leave them to die in the snow?'

In the silence that followed, Georgette fell asleep and never found out why the woman thought they would be blamed if Robert died.

*

They stayed with their benefactors, who introduced themselves as Mollin and Anita, for five days. For the first two, Robert was too weak to talk; almost too weak to sip the sweetened warm milk the woman gave Georgette to slip between his lips. On the third day, he was able to rise from his straw pallet and walk, with support, to sit on a bench before the fire and murmur his thanks for every attention. On the fourth, he proclaimed he was well enough to take a walk outdoors, but his hosts said it was too snowy that day and he had better stay in the house. Georgette too was dissuaded from helping with outdoor farm chores 'to avoid becoming cold and falling ill with whatever had ailed the young man'. So she built up her strength in the warm hut, caring for Robert and doing what she could to assist her hosts indoors by way of cooking and cleaning and spinning. She had never stayed in a hut with a chimney before and she loved watching the smoke from the hearth spiral up into a dark hole and disappear like magic.

On the fifth day, Robert announced that he would be strong enough to depart with Georgette the following morning.

The man looked at him doubtfully. 'Perhaps one more day of rest, to be sure?'

But Robert and Georgette were in accord, as always. Those who waited for them had waited too long. They must relieve that anxiety by reaching home as soon as possible. And they longed for home more passion-ately as they drew closer and closer. Perhaps two weeks of travel remained, depending on their pace. Only two weeks, after all the terrible months.

That was the day the woman suspended her largest iron pot from the pot hanger in the fireplace and heated water in it. She hung a blanket from the ceiling in one corner of the hut and then helped the man to carry inside a huge cauldron that they placed behind the blanket, creating a private area. Robert and Georgette watched with interest as the man carried behind the curtain first several buckets of hot water and then a bucket or two of cold water from the well.

'Come, young Robert,' the man said. 'I will help you to bathe.'

Robert disappeared behind the curtain and Georgette heard plenty of splashing. When he emerged, he was pink and shiny, wound in a blanket that had been warming near the fire. Then the woman took Georgette behind the curtain. Robert marvelled at the sheen in her loose, flowing hair when she too was escorted back to the hearth, dressed in her own shift that had been scrubbed and stiffened with flour-water the previous day. It was the first time each of them had ever washed their entire body at one time, other than by swimming in a river, and they felt wonderfully fresh.

Their hosts carried the cauldron outside and apparently took their own baths, for they fairly gleamed when they returned, the man in a long white tunic and the woman in an embroidered white shift.

'We shall have a special dinner tonight. Your last night with us,' announced the woman, spreading a clean piece of linen over the trestle table and bringing out not one but two candles. The wine was sweet and served in a single silver-coloured goblet that they passed from hand to hand. The man and woman's lips moved before they drank their share, and Georgette wondered if they were making a secret wish perhaps. For herself, she wished that apple cider had been served rather than wine: the pullet the woman had roasted was so salty that she had to drink mug after mug to quench her thirst.

After dinner, the man turned to Robert.

'Is it possible you know the game of chess, young Robert?'

Smiling, Robert answered in the affirmative. 'Some years ago, there was a nobleman forced to stay at my abbey for a few weeks because of a broken leg. He was most impatient at the inactivity and for his amusement he taught me the rules of chess and we played every day. But I have not had any partner since, and I forget the rules.'

As excited as a boy who has found another boy to play ball with, the man dismissed Robert's diffidence and brought out a board and ornate wooden pieces he had carved himself. They played for a long time, the man advising Robert during the first few games before settling into serious play.

Her head heavy from too much wine, Georgette lay down on her pallet as soon as she had finished helping to clear the table after dinner. Within minutes, she was asleep. Robert glanced back to smile at her snoring and caught sight of the woman, who was standing at a small window on the far side of the room with a scarf of lacework draped over her hair, reciting a prayer of some kind with her eyes closed. How strange, Robert thought, that she prays standing rather than kneeling, and does not uncover her hair.

At that moment, the woman opened her eyes and saw Robert observing her.

'Would you, would you care for some more wine, young Robert?' she asked hastily.

When Robert demurred, she muttered a goodnight and disappeared behind the curtain, hiding the marital bed.

Robert's subsequent distraction lost him that game. To his host's disappointment, he declined an invitation to play again, claiming weariness. Soon the house was quiet and dark.

In the morning Georgette woke a little late. Their hosts were not in the house, perhaps out feeding their animals. Robert was lying still on his mattress, staring blankly, lost in thought. She knew him so well; something was troubling him.

Georgette rose quietly and sat down cross-legged beside him, pulling her blanket around her for warmth. He was looking up at the ceiling of the little farmhouse, his hands linked behind his head.

'What is it, Robert?' she whispered.

When he finally replied, he didn't look at her. It was as if he was talking to himself. 'They're Jews.'

Georgette started. These kind people were of the same creed as the hordes that shouted sweet Jesus to his death? She winced as she remembered Gregor's description of beating Jews the night before he grew ill. He said they had put a curse upon him and indeed he never recovered. But maybe it was cruelly beating a man, a man who looked not too different from their father, which had haunted him. It was the first time he had measured the man behind the Jew, and this was her first time. The measurements didn't fit.

They left after a breakfast of bread and cheese in front of an unlit hearth. Their hosts led them directly from the door into the woods, guiding them along what they said was a quick path through the forest to the market road, where passing farmers might offer them a ride. Robert and Georgette followed obediently; it seemed clear that their hosts did not want them to see any of the other people in the village, or perhaps they did not want their neighbours to see their young guests.

'You saved my life. I will always be deeply grateful,' Robert said when they reached the market road. He looked into the man's eyes and then those of the woman, and grasped their hands in turn. 'May God bless you.'

The woman smiled and turned to Georgette, who blushed and stammered. Looking down, she murmured her thanks again and again, until the woman stopped her with a brief touch on the arm.

There was an awkward silence.

'Off you go, then,' the man said. 'May God be with you too.'

As they turned away, he lifted his hand and Georgette had a wild fear that the heretic was casting a spell on them. But glancing behind her, she saw he was simply waving, and she waved back. Then the two couples turned their backs and walked in opposite directions.

CHAPTER NINETEEN

As Robert and Georgette drew closer to her village, she became almost giddy with longing for home, for the sweet scent of a new straw roof, for the sights and sounds of the whole village working together to bring in the wheat harvest. If Bess had not been slaughtered in the fall, would the fat old sow recognise her? She dared not wonder about the health of her father and beloved Father David. She had been away for a year, but she wanted desperately for everything to be unchanged. Yet without Gregor, how could things ever be the same?

When they were about a mile away, she led Robert off the main track and along the borders between the small fields, taking care not to trespass on the fallow earth as it emerged from winter's blanket. They zigzagged in a roundabout way until they had circled the village at a distance and arrived at the back of the little hamlet.

'We will be able to reach my father's house unseen from here,' Georgette said. 'So the old crones who sit in the square watching everyone's business will not send a messenger to my father before I can reach him myself. Perhaps busybodies live to such a ripe old age because the saints dread to welcome their gossiping tongues into the peace of Heaven.'

Robert grinned. 'Even in the monastery we had old crones in skirts, but they were male.'

'I used to take this path after Easter Mass or on feast days, not to avoid the gossips but to avoid the young louts who loitered in the square after Mass. They wouldn't do much to me, but they loved to provoke Gregor into a rage. So I used to tell him I wanted to stretch my legs after the service, and sometimes it would work and he would accompany me.'

Her voice trembled. The familiar surroundings gave rise to vivid memories of her brother, and she was sick at the thought of telling her father he no longer had a son. *Please, God, may I have a father still*, she thought.

Georgette led them behind two houses and paused at the third. The mortar of clay, dung and straw covering the woven strips of wood that made up their walls was crumbling, and she could see the reason. The tree saplings her father had planted where walls joined each other had been allowed to diverge from their slow job of sealing the joint. Upstart side branches were trying to push the walls apart like the arms of blind Samson in the temple of the Philistines. The yard was overgrown with weeds.

Georgette tidied her skirt and smoothed her hair, but still she hesitated. Robert gave her a gentle push towards the hut. He walked a few yards away and occupied himself with unpacking his bundle.

Slowly, she opened the door. Sitting in front of the fire with his elbow on the table and his head resting wearily on his hand, was her father. His back was towards the door and clearly he had not heard her enter, for he sat motionless.

Swallowing, Georgette glanced around. The hut was dirty and unkempt. Her father's cracked leather working boots lay next to him, although she had always been firm that he and Gregor must remove their boots and leave them at the door so as not to bring the muck of the farm and lanes inside. There was only one lonely salted ham hanging from the rafters, and a string of sausages she herself had smoked shortly before she left. The half-loaf of bread on the table was misshapen and under-baked.

As a sob caught in her throat, her father heard the sound and turned round. She did not remember that his eyes had been poor, yet he looked at her and squinted, then looked again.

Slowly, he stood up, a man who was still in his thirties but already old from unrelenting work . . . and the disappearance of his children. Georgette dared not approach him. But he hurried towards her, reached out wonderingly to touch her face, and grabbed her in a tight clasp such as she had never received from him before.

'Georgette, Georgette,' he cried and she cried too. For a moment they were complete.

Suddenly, she felt his body stiffen and she knew that he was looking for Gregor behind her.

'I am so sorry, Father. I could not save him,' she cried. He held her at arm's length to see her face, his eyes begging for a different outcome.

'He had the ague,' she sobbed. 'He coughed blood. I made a physic for him and he drank it. I tried to keep him warm. But in the morning his body was cold. I am so sorry, Father.'

'Aagh,' he grunted, covering his face with his hands. Apprehensively, Georgette stroked his bent shoulders. Would he blame her? Would the pain be too much for him?

Her father closed her in his arms again. Together they grieved for the strong, fiery, angry, lost Gregor.

After a while, Georgette released herself gently. 'Father,' she said, 'God has been good to me. I was alone after Gregor died and He gave me a true friend. I wish to introduce to you my friend, my protector, my . . . betrothed, Robert of the Abbey of Blois.'

Lifting her voice, she called Robert's name and bade him enter. Her father turned, his mouth open at her words and at the sight of a young man of indeterminate age – from his face, a youth, but from his demeanour, a man. Georgette was a child. Who could possibly have arranged her betrothal without his permission? But before he could say anything, his words were arrested by Robert's steady gaze. As if the youth could read his mind, his first words addressed the older man's consternation.

'I am honoured to meet Georgette's father, sir. Had these been ordinary times, I would have asked my guardian, the Abbot of Blois, to approach you first and ask your permission that I might have your daughter's hand in marriage. I pray that you will forgive our unorthodox engagement and bless our union.'

Georgette's father measured the youth for a long time and turned to his daughter. The girl's cheeks were glowing at the words of her chosen. She was a child no more. And the boy, or man, or something different from both, so unusual was he, waited respectfully for her father's answer.

Slowly, Georgette's father took her hands and joined them with the boy's hands. He lifted his own arms above their heads and said simply, 'You have my blessing. And thanks be to God for bringing you home safely to me.'

There were more tears for Gregor, just a few stories about their terrible journey, and some toasting of the betrothal with a sharp, burning liquid from a bottle Georgette's father had hidden in the house.

'And now, Father,' Georgette said, her voice shaky with dread. 'What of Father David. Is he well?'

'My daughter, be strong.' Her father hesitated. 'Father David is in Heaven now.'

Georgette's eyes widened. She shook her head.

'It was quite soon after you left,' replied her father. 'The village women who tended him on his deathbed say he spoke of the Crusade. He said the Crusade was ungodly madness and he should have tried to stop it. But others said that was sacrilege, and he must have gone out of his mind or he would not have said such bad things.'

The saintly priest had been one of the first victims of the Children's Crusade. He had seen the truth, and it had killed him. No, she, Georgette, had killed him.

Georgette cried for a long time, turning first to her father and then to Robert, but there was no comforting her.

CHAPTER TWENTY

The next day was a hard one. It was impossible to evade the questions of the families of the young Crusaders, so they had to face the harsh duty of telling several parents that their wandering children would never return. One small headstone for Patrice and another for Gregor were placed next to the simple gravestone of the priest. Around all three, Georgette planted the old man's favourite flowers, pale yellow primroses and mauve loosestrife.

There was a different service the following day, a simple but sweet wedding for the young couple in the church where she had grown up under the care of the old priest. The bride and groom declined the traditional dancing and gay music after the ceremony, but a hastily baked bridal cake and horns of bride-ale were served in the village square.

Finally, four days after their arrival in the village, Georgette and Robert departed again, bound for the Abbey of Blois.

Georgette's father embraced Robert before they left.

'I don't want to lose another son,' he explained as he shamefacedly wiped tears from his face.

'But remember, Father, you are to come and live with us in our home as soon as I have found work,' said Robert.

Georgette dashed back into her father's arms for yet another embrace. 'I will never abandon you again. Never,' she pledged.

A merchant travelling their way made space for the newly-weds in his cart. They carefully positioned the priest's chest of precious manuscripts. The priest had written a simple will when he became sick, leaving his eight or ten beloved books to Georgette. She knew nothing of their considerable value in gold, but she was overwhelmed by their value in learning. For she and Robert were equally determined that she would continue her own studies, beginning with the wealth she now owned.

Georgette sat on the cart, her anxiety spoiling the novel ride. *Such a learned man will surely find my simple background an unsatisfactory match for his protégé.* She became more nervous when they reached the lands owned by the Abbey of Blois, stretching green and vast ahead of them. *He is the abbot of a great monastery, and I am but a peasant girl.* In another mood, she would have enjoyed the orderliness of the fields, the tall trees, the entrance with its soaring pointed arch. *So different from the poor home of my beloved priest.*

Her anxiety was premature. The abbot no longer resided at Blois. He had been summoned from the abbey to Paris, where he was to assist the judges of the standing council in the ecclesiastical court.

''Tis a great honour for Père Abbé,' the friendly monk at the door of the monastery told them. He had greeted Robert first formally in Latin, and then affectionately in a simple country French, and he spoke French thereafter for Georgette's benefit. He insisted on leading them to join the midday repast in the great refectory, where the monks served daily meals to the poor. Now they sat in the huge echoing hall, and many people came up to welcome Robert back and to exclaim at his brief, edited summary of their journey.

Robert had told Georgette of the jolly twin cooks who provided a lonely young boy with the only ounce of spoiling he received. Now he asked permission, suddenly shy, to enter the great kitchen and introduce his new wife to them.

Their host hesitated. 'They disappeared,' he said.

The young couple looked at him blankly.

The monk glanced around to check if anyone was nearby and leaned closer. 'We are not supposed to talk about it, but an apprentice cook reported to the abbot that, for a fortnight or longer, the twins had been spending excessive time every day talking with a traveller from the south. A very poor-looking fellow, he reported, ragged and wearing rough wooden shoes. The apprentice said the stranger sometimes read to them from a book written in a dialect similar to ours. Couldn't have been the Holy Bible because it was not in Latin, but the few words he could catch were about Lord Jesus.'

The monk glanced around again before continuing.

'The abbot summoned the twins and ordered them to send the stranger packing. A few days later, the twins were gone too. After nigh on twenty years in the kitchen here.'

The bells rang and the monk hurried off, urging them to hasten lest they be late for prayer.

'What words about Lord Jesus could a stranger offer that would be strong enough to draw two monks from their abbey?' Georgette mused, turning to Robert.

But his face was stricken. 'I wanted to thank them,' he whispered.

Georgette was not reluctant to have her meeting with the august personage delayed. But Robert was anxious about the possible effect of Abbot Benedict's new posting on his own future. They slept at the abbey that night, in separate rooms as was the rule, but left early the next morning to take advantage of a ride to Paris with a farmer who was taking a wagonload of ducks that had been specially ordered for a feast.

'Do they not have a market in the whole city of Paris where they could find ducks more easily?' Georgette asked.

'Aye,' the farmer told her as his horse trotted along, 'but some folks are so rich that they care which breed of ducks they serve their guests. They are willing to pay for the transportation from another place if such birds are not available at the market when they need them. Plus an extra charge I add simply because I've discovered they'll pay it!' the farmer said with a smile of satisfaction at his business acumen.

Georgette watched the ducks as they squawked in their wooden crates. Certainly, they were plump and glossily healthy, but could someone really taste the difference between the flesh of one fat duck and another?

The gates of the city came into view. Georgette whispered a prayer for her brother, who had not been spared to enter the city he so wished to see. She could not believe her luck when the cart passed under the heavy portcullis without a word from the guards. She was inside one of the greatest cities in Christendom. She, little Georgette from the village of Illiers, was in Paris.

The smell of the city assailed her first. Her nostrils wrinkled at the strong odour of sewage running down the street. And she felt oppressed by the buildings rising steeply on either side of the street, soaring to Heaven yet blocking out that heavenly light. What a great amount of stone must have been quarried to build such towers – enough to leave a black hole in the earth as big as the city.

The noise frightened her: the clamour of so many voices talking at once. Surely, they could not all hear one another. Probably that was why they shouted, like the fishmonger and the butcher in her village market. No, she did not like the city at all. She clung to Robert's hand and moved closer to him.

With a tug on the reins, the cart driver stopped outside a pair of forbidding gates.

'Are we here already?' she said weakly.

Robert tried to smile. 'Apparently so.'

They carried their bundles, as they had done for so long, and entered the abbey in which, they had been told, Abbot Benedict had made his home. Small by the standards of an abbey in the countryside, it seemed enormous in the city, towering over the neighbouring buildings and surrounded by a wall so thick two men could sleep side by side atop it and not worry about rolling off in the night. If Georgette had not been so wrapped in apprehension, she would have been dazzled by the magnificent stonework, the details of the gargoyles, and the sheer bulk of the building.

A young monk whom they asked for directions took them down long cloisters, with stonework as adeptly sculpted as any statue, through several courtyards, past a large kitchen, and down a shallow flight of stairs to a series of low openings lining a dark passageway.

'Abbot Benedict lives here, in the furthest one of these meditation cells,' he said, pointing, 'although the Lord knows that he could choose to stay in comfortable, warm rooms upstairs. The title of his first sermon at this abbey was "Comfort Weakens the Spirit" and certainly his spirit must have grown stronger in this damp, dark cave. Well, I must return to my duties now. Fare thee well in the name of Christ our Lord.'

'Wait here,' Robert said, guiding Georgette to a stone bench near the cell. 'I will first prepare him before I introduce you.' There was a tension in Robert's manner that made Georgette more uneasy. Calm, steady Robert, in whose face she had never before seen fear, was nervous and apprehensive.

With a slight straightening of his shoulders, Robert stood before the last gate and tapped on the bars.

CHAPTER TWENTY-ONE

'*Veni*,' came a cold, clear order in Latin. Robert swung open the gate, ducked his head below the low entryway, and disappeared from Georgette's view.

Georgette remembered Father David telling her that the discipline in the monastery where he spent his first years as a priest was so strict that there was only an opening, or at most a gate to each cell, so that the actions of the monk within could be seen by anyone walking by. Georgette could not see from where she sat, but every word was clearly audible to her.

After a pause, a voice said, 'Can it be? I cannot see you clearly in the dark and you are not wearing your hood. Robert, is that you? Have you indeed returned safely from your pilgrimage?'

'I have returned, Père Abbé,' Robert replied shakily.

Georgette heard a chair pushed back and a few rapid

footsteps, then there was another pause and she imagined the youth and the older man embracing.

'Thanks be to our Lord,' the abbot exclaimed finally. 'I am shamed that I almost lost faith in God's will to bring you back to me. When I was summoned to the city, I left word that if you returned, the monks at Blois must send you to join me here in Paris. And so it has happened. Glory be to our Lord. Come and sit here by the fire, Robert.'

There was a creaking of stools. 'I am glad to find you well, and congratulate you on the honour accorded to you by the Church,' Robert said, and Georgette wondered at the formality between the two.

'I am humbled by the trust accorded me by my superiors,' the abbot replied. 'But tell me of your travels, boy. Did you see the Lord's holy city?'

'No, Père Abbé,' came Robert's quiet reply. 'We reached only as far as Marseilles. There, our leader, after promising miracles in the name of the Lord, deserted us, and two merchants deceived a large number of young Crusaders into slavery. Along the way to Marseilles, we met with kindness from villagers who blessed our pilgrimage, but we also saw self-righteous savagery against those not of our faith, which wounded me deeply. Many was the time when I wished for your counsel as I witnessed godlessness on a journey taken in God's name.'

There was no reply from Robert's mentor. After a moment, he began to recite a Hail Mary in a monotone, his beads clicking furiously as he chanted. Another Hail Mary followed, and a third, before he spoke.

'I am sorry for your pain and struggle. I must urge you, though, to accept that the task of spreading the law of God might entail some actions that do not lie comfortably in bed with the soul. Enforcing that law is our highest task and we must not flinch from its execution.'

There was only silence from Robert, and Georgette understood how such a response must have disappointed him deeply.

The abbot changed the subject. 'I will have a cell prepared for you next to mine, my boy. I wish I had known of your arrival. When did you return to our area?'

'Last week,' Robert replied woodenly. 'But I spent the first few days in the village of Illiers, where it was my most painful duty to inform several families of the loss of their children. There is much anger there against the leader of our expedition, who disappeared in Marseilles, and many swore to travel to his home village and to hang his father for encouraging him in leading young people to their death.'

The abbot tried again to return to safer ground. 'But why did you go to Illiers first, Robert? That is a long detour from the road to our old abbey.'

Georgette twisted her skirt nervously. Now she would be introduced to the abbot.

'I went to pay my respects to the father of the girl I planned to wed. She is from that village and joined the pilgrimage along with her brother, who died, like many others along the way. Our presence was needed to console the father. And he was consoled indeed by our quiet wedding last Sabbath.'

'Your wedding?' the abbot repeated in an angry voice. 'You are married? You, who was to marry the Church, as I did, and to serve only the Lord for ever? I cannot believe what you are saying! For a mere village girl, you have thrown away a brilliant career in the Church. Nay, Robert, tell me that it was a poor jest. Tell me that you are pure still and prepared to rise in the service of the Church as I have planned since your childhood.'

As Georgette sat frozen with horror, Robert's voice replied, as level and courteous as he could make it, but firm and cool. 'My wife waits for your blessing outside your chamber, Père Abbé. I hope we shall not upset her with such lack of welcome.'

The abbot's reply was inaudible. Clearly, he was now aware of a larger audience for his words. For a few minutes Georgette heard only sibilant hissing from the abbot, and finally Robert appeared in the doorway. His face was white, but he walked without hesitation towards her and took her hand to lead her inside. When she shrank from entering, he lifted her hand to his lips and kissed it firmly, and then he drew her inside.

A tall, skeletal figure sat before the fire, clothed entirely in black, fingering his rosary beads automatically. He said nothing at Georgette's approach but observed her silently, his face hard and angry. The sockets of his eyes were sunken and dark, as if he habitually slept and ate little. He must have been a refined and handsome man in his youth, but the lack of fat on his bones made his features look sharp and forbidding now.

Georgette curtsied and kept her eyes lowered, but her cheeks were flushed – not with shame but with anger at the man's rudeness. Instinctively she steeled herself to show no nervousness or fear of this man. As he had been for many years the teacher and mentor of her husband, she would be respectful in her manner, but she would not be cowed by his fury at her presence here beside Robert. *I am the wife of my husband*, she told herself. *And I was once the pupil of a good priest as learned as any abbot, and apparently many times as kind as this particular one.*

'Robert, take your . . . wife to the kitchen and tell the priest in charge there that you are to be given a hot meal and . . . suitable sleeping accommodation. I will talk with you tomorrow morn,' said the abbot, rising abruptly and turning from them as he moved away to a plain desk and sat down there, his back as rigid as the plank chair.

'Goodnight, Père Abbé,' Robert said in a low but steady voice, and Georgette forced herself to dip a slight curtsy and turned to follow her husband.

Silently, they exited the main building and made their way across a raked-sand courtyard to the huge kitchen they had passed only fifteen minutes earlier. But just before entering the kitchen, they turned aside in silent agreement and sat down together on a stone bench in the herb garden.

'I apologise on the abbot's behalf,' Robert began, in a stiff voice. Georgette barely recognised his strange way of speaking and his strained white face. This wasn't the Robert she knew, who was always so confident and open in her company.

'Don't, my love,' she burst out, taking his face between his hands. 'You need not say sorry to me. Indeed, it is I who am sorry for you.'

Without replying, he turned and buried his head in her shoulder, like a lost child seeking comfort. They sat close together like that for a few minutes, amid the soothing scents of lavender and rosemary, before entering the building.

PART FOUR

A Journey of Learning

Chapter Twenty-Two

Georgette smiled at the funny sight the ducks presented as they stuck their necks between the bars of their cages, bobbed their heads up and down, and quacked angrily at the passers-by. They seemed to feel that, if they protested and scolded their owners loudly enough, they might be returned to freedom. As each chicken, each turkey, and each pigeon at the Friday morning market in the great cobbled square had the same erroneous idea, the air was alive with squalls, honks, clucks and hoots.

The daily market on the right bank of Paris bore little resemblance to the modest and comparatively seemly gathering that had been termed a market in her home village. Here, fish hawkers thrust their slimy catch boldly near the faces of shoppers, dangling strange creatures of the deep that seemed to leer around the hooks in their mouths. Sweating men carrying impossible loads cursed those who blocked their path in words as salty as any sailor's. Straw tossed on the ground was clotted with the blood of newly slaughtered carcasses, while a sour smell emanated from rotting produce and the sewerage that flowed undirected along the sides of the narrow alleys.

Georgette spent almost exactly the amount of money she had planned and rolled the last few coins into a tiny piece of cloth that she tucked down her bosom. She thanked God every day for the impression that a younger Robert had made on the rector of the university years earlier, when the boy had navigated the university's vast library without assistance. Despite the former Abbot of Blois' silence on the matter of his former protégé, or perhaps because of it, the rector had accepted Robert into the university on a scholarship. Because Robert was married – a most unusual circumstance among students at the university – and must support a wife, the rector had even arranged for Robert to assist in the library, earning payment just sufficient for the rent of their little room. Georgette's hours of spinning wool for the shopkeeper on the ground floor brought them a few coins, and with painstaking management, she kept them not richly but quite adequately fed.

As for the abbot, he had shown no hint of forgiveness or conciliation in the six months they had lived in Paris. Robert had returned to see him, as bidden, on the morning after their arrival, hoping the abbot had come to some measure of acceptance. But the abbot's anger and passion had grown stronger overnight.

'I can barely believe what you told me yesterday, boy. Word of your ridiculous marriage, your break from the path I set for you, will make me a laughing stock for those who watched me educate and guide you. You cannot do this to me. I demand that you swear before God, right now, that you will have this village wedding annulled, which it is in my power to arrange, and to join the Church in a suitable position, which it is also within my power to arrange.'

Robert stared at him. 'My wife is my life, Père Abbé. Without her, I would have died, first in my soul and later in my body.'

'Bah, sentimental nonsense, boy,' the abbot roared, rising and looming over Robert. 'I am the one to whom you owe this life of yours. I picked you from the gutter. I saved you from an early grave. You were dust and I gave you form.'

Then Robert too was on his feet, his face flushed and his eyes flashing. 'You were my saviour indeed, my teacher and my guide, and I will never forget the enormous debt I owe you. And perhaps some day I will pass on your great favours to an unfortunate youth in need. But when he is grown, I will not, I could not, tell him what he is to be. That he must learn for himself.'

'Do not dare to talk back to me, boy. If you do not obey me, I will cut you off for ever.'

There! The threat was spoken. There was silence, broken only by the quick angry breaths of both men.

Robert spoke quietly, 'When I told you, Père Abbé, that God had it in His mind that I join the Children's Crusade, I was right, but not in the way I understood at the time. That terrible journey, which affected me more deeply than you permitted me to share with you last night, was my first glimpse of a long and winding path God intends me to take.

'And without detracting from my gratitude to you, Père Abbé, I follow the path of God.' Robert bent, took up his cape from the bench, wished the abbot God's blessings, and left.

The two had not met since. Georgette did not lament the loss of a powerful sponsor, but she was sad for Robert, who had not been welcomed home as she had. She knew he missed the abbot's protection, his guidance and experience.

'Brooding old blackbird. His brain got so big that he sacrificed his heart to make space for it. But he cannot get between my husband and me. We share two hearts that beat as one,' Georgette muttered. 'I will not darken this beautiful day with thoughts of the abbot.'

Her basket held fish, a small loaf of bread, a little

cheese, two sprigs of tansy for their straw mattress to discourage fleas, and, balancing carefully on the top, a treat: raspberries almost as fat as the ones she used to gather from wild canes at home. Robert loved raspberries, and she had bargained well for them.

On her way home, after she crossed the bridge to the Île de la Cité and turned into the narrow alley where she and Robert lived, Georgette remembered to cross the road before passing a certain tall house. The neighbour who rented the top floor had a habit of dropping her slops from the upstairs window without a shout of warning.

Once she reached her own tiny home on the upper floor of a narrow timber house, she placed her purchases on the rough table and began to put the room to rights. Humming, she punched the straw mattress, shook the bed quilt, dusted fluffy ends of wool from her spindle and distaff, swept the floor, spread fresh straw, and scrubbed the table. She arranged the plump and fuzzy raspberries on a perfect, glowing-green oak leaf she had picked on her way from the market – God's beauty.

Taking the chamber pot from under the bed, Georgette called a warning out of the window and waited an exaggerated time for any reply before emptying out the contents. She winced as the sewage joined the putrid rivulet below, and a pig waddled closer to sample the swill. On hot days, children splashed in the foul stream. She and her father had shaken their heads about this aspect of Paris. In the village, they recalled together, people threw their waste into a deep pit, and dug another when that one was full. When charcoal was scattered in regularly, the pit hardly smelled at all.

During the far too short but blessed three months that her father had lived with them before he fell ill and died, father and daughter had walked the streets, like the country folk they were, gawking at the tall buildings, pointing out the fine carriages, wondering at the luxurious goods for sale.

Their favourite stroll took them to a viewing place on the bank of the Seine. On the opposite side, hundreds of workers swarmed around a massive half-completed stone structure with a strangely beautiful shape. The outer walls shot true up to the sky, then curved gracefully towards each other and kissed at the sharp point at the top. It was a palace of a cathedral, a soaring, sacred building, called Notre Dame.

Tears came to Georgette's eyes at the memory. 'We were happy together, Father, weren't we?' she whispered.

Once she had cleaned the room, Georgette spent two quiet hours at her spinning. Then it was time to heat Robert's pottage over the little stove. To save the money it would cost him to eat the midday meal in an alehouse, as many of the other students did, she always took his food to him, wrapping the warm bowl in linen cloths.

'Tell me about your morning classes, Robert,' she said, as they sat in a sunny corner of the great courtyard just inside the university walls and dipped their horn spoons into the same bowl.

'There was a debate about the order that Brother Francis started,' he said, and her eyes lit up. The experience they had shared the previous year, the journey that had made them everything to each other, had at the same time made them different from everyone else, it seemed. Their faith had been burned in a fire, beaten on an anvil, and emerged changed. Even at the university, where a new discipline, the formal study of theology, was taking shape, Robert had found no scholar who shared the exact timbre of his beliefs. Only the teachings of Brother Francis of Assisi came anywhere close.

'Our teacher said that the Pope was right to tonsure Brother Francis and his disciples against their will, for a monk's shaven head is a sign of submission to the Church.'

'Did they explain why Brother Francis objected . . . ?'

But as Georgette began her question, they were both distracted by a little knot of students who had gathered around a stranger quite near them. He looked foreign, not only because of his unfamiliar cassock but for his dark complexion and strange accent. His voice was clear and it had carried to them a fragment that drew them to their feet and closer to his story.

'Child slaves, French child slaves, I tell you.'

'And you stood by as this happened?' demanded one student.

Pain crossed the stranger's face like a shadow, and his voice cracked as he defended himself.

'I tried, indeed I did. When I heard the children utter some words in French, I went closer and asked them how they had come to such a sad plight. They said they were pilgrims on their way from Marseilles to the Holy Land. But they were captured by pirates and sold as slaves instead.

'I begged the slave owners to release them to my custody. I said they were children of my faith and promised to reimburse them if they would give me a little time to raise the money from my community. They laughed at me and said I could never come up with enough money.

'"These are not just ordinary slaves,"' they boasted to me. "It is rare to find a group of such attractive child slaves, European children." It was clear that they expected to make a fortune from the sale.

'When I persisted and threatened to seek the

intervention of a certain Christian courtier in the employ of the sultan, they set upon me. They hit me over the head and dumped me, unconscious, beyond the city walls. By the time I came to, and ran to my superiors for help, the children had been sold and their captors had disappeared.'

Robert's voice broke harshly into the group's exclamations of disgust.

'How long ago did you see these child slaves and where?'

''Twas but a few months ago, in my home country of Egypt, in the port of Alexandria, where slave auctions are held perhaps two times in each week.'

'How many were there?'

'Some hundreds, I would calculate. They said they were more at the start, enough to fill seven ships, but two ships were lost in a storm. The remaining five ships were met by pirates, ruffians who, strangely, seemed familiar to the crew. The children were chained to one another and transferred on to boats bound for the slave market.'

The students in the group were staring at Robert, who was usually silent and aloof, as he snapped his terse questions. Turning away abruptly, he drew Georgette quickly out of the courtyard and to a quiet corner so they could be alone.

The young couple never spoke about the Children's Crusade. They would have shrunk from exposing to anyone else the cataclysm of that journey. And they felt no need to talk to each other about an experience they shared so intimately. Now, suddenly, the tragic conclusion of the Children's Crusade felt raw and terrible again.

'Patrice,' Georgette whispered. 'And the others. Tied up like animals, in a faraway land.' Wild, independent Patrice. Or maybe she was dead at the bottom of the sea, pale young flesh nibbled by creatures of the deep. Georgette sobbed as she had sobbed only for the death of her brother and that of Father David. Robert held her tightly.

CHAPTER TWENTY-THREE

One evening, not long after the encounter with the stranger, there was a firm knock on their door. The couple glanced at each other; they knew no one who would visit at this hour.

Making his voice stern, Robert called out through the locked door, 'Who goes there?'

'My name is Brother Thomas. I was a friend of Father David of Illiers many years ago.'

Robert turned to Georgette but she was already at the door, her fingers clumsy in their haste to open the bolt.

An old man dressed in the same humble black habit Father David had worn and the same rough wooden shoes was standing on the threshold with a tentative smile on his face. There was an openness and simplicity in his expression she had not seen since she left Father David for the Crusade.

'Please enter, Brother Thomas,' she said, drawing him inside. 'I am Georgette and this is my husband, Robert.' Robert offered their guest a seat close to the fire and handed him the mug of hot cider, which he had not yet had a chance to drink.

'How in the name of the Lord did you find out that I was a friend of Father David?' Georgette asked, her voice breaking over the dear name.

Brother Thomas stretched out his feet to the fire and murmured his thanks for the warming drink. 'I had not been near Father David's adopted village for many years, ever since we parted as young men, so when I found myself in the district I walked a good distance to visit my old friend. It was a great sadness to me that he had died in the meantime.'

Georgette bowed her head.

'When I asked about his books, I was told that he had left them to a young girl he had helped to raise, and that the girl had married a man called Robert, who was studying at the University of Paris. That was some months ago. It happened that my work brought me to Paris this morning. I asked some questions of the students at the university, and this evening I followed my man home. Please forgive me for not approaching you directly, young Robert, but my business is with your wife and I thought it best to speak to her directly.'

Robert nodded and Georgette asked, 'What is your errand, good brother?'

'Father David owned some copies of the Gospel translated into vernacular French,' he replied. 'These copies are very useful for . . . a certain purpose of which he approved. I hope to presume upon your generosity in requesting that you allow me to take the books with me on my travels.'

Robert and Georgette stared at him. Those two books were copied simply without decoration, but they were nevertheless valuable. It was an extraordinary request from a stranger.

'I think we can talk about that business after dinner,' Georgette prevaricated. 'If you only arrived in Paris this morning and have been trailing my husband since then, you cannot have eaten. And following a man secretly is very tiring, I would imagine.'

Brother Thomas flushed, but she smiled back to show him she bore him no malice. Meekly he accepted her invitation to join them at the little trestle table for hot pottage and Georgette's excellent honey mead.

There was no meekness in Brother Thomas's conversation after dinner. He was passionate and articulate.

'When Father David and I were studying at the seminary together, we drew close to a teacher whom we greatly respected. He told us about the ideas of a man called

Peter Waldes, a nobleman from the town of Lyons who gave away all his earthly possessions forty years before Brother Frances of Assisi did so more publicly.

'People who follow his creed are called Waldensians by outsiders. We prefer the name the Poor of Christ. I left the seminary before I was ordained and joined that community. Father David was greatly drawn to these beliefs too, but he told me our Mother Church was the only mother he had ever had, and he owed it to her to obey her faithfully.'

Georgette thought of the look on Father David's face when she left on the Crusade. For his loyalty to the Church he had paid a high price in pain and regret.

'Why are those French translations of the Gospel so important to you that you follow them all the way to our home?' Robert asked.

'Some of us among the Poor of Christ do not stay in one place but travel the country, preaching discreetly to those who seem sympathetic. We need copies of the Gospels in the French spoken by the people so that everyone can understand what is written. The Gospels in Latin seem but magical incantations to illiterate peasants. Priests benefit from the role of magicians who are the intermediaries between God and the people.

'We want to reveal the treasure of Christ to everyone, instead of hoarding its jewels for only a few.'

Georgette and Robert alighted on the same memory.

'The twin cooks at the abbey,' she murmured.

'They were drawn to the stranger with the book about Jesus in French,' he confirmed.

They talked far into the night, the glowing fire sending sparks flying up into the shadows. Brother Thomas drew a picture of the beliefs and practices of the Poor of Christ that closely mirrored the understanding Robert and Georgette had reached through their sufferings on the Crusade. Finally there was someone they could confide in.

Robert had never forgiven Abbot Benedict for being unwilling or unable to talk to him about his anguish and confusion. Slowly, then in a flood of words, he unburdened himself to a very different teacher.

'On that journey,' he ended finally, 'I saw the appetite for violence disguised as duty to God, hatred of others disguised as love of God. But those people are as sure of their rightness as I am. How can I know for sure what is right?'

Brother Thomas took Robert by his shoulders and gently guided him to the floor, to his knees. He knelt beside him.

'O God,' he prayed aloud. 'Heal the soul of this boy who has seen the evil of man falsely committed in Your name. Comfort him. And teach him to ask only one question when he is uncertain: "What would my son Jesus have done when He walked on Earth?" Amen.'

The old man put his arms around Robert just as Father David had comforted Georgette as a child, and Robert cried.

'The Poor of Christ do not believe in violence,' Brother Thomas elaborated as they settled before the fire again. 'The Crusades by their very purpose are violent. When Sister Sabrina was preaching last week, she –'

'You have women preachers?' exclaimed Robert and Georgette simultaneously.

'Indeed we do, for the Word may emerge as clearly from a woman's mouth as from a man's.'

Georgette lost the thread of the conversation for a while after that, her mind busy with thoughts she had never confessed, even to Robert. Why couldn't she study at a great school? Why couldn't she sit in the library at the university and have access to the riches of books there? She had a sudden image of herself preaching to a small group of men and women. Blushing at her own hubris, she returned her attention to her guest.

'What about those who will not believe in Jesus Christ?' Robert was asking the priest. 'The Jews, the Muslims, the unbelievers of the world?'

'They are not unbelievers; they have different beliefs,'

Brother Thomas said. 'We pray that they will find their way to Jesus Christ, but such a path cannot be forced. As long as they believe in the kingship of God, they will pursue lives of good deeds. Jesus would wish us to love them for that alone.'

Eventually, Brother Thomas had to take his leave. He believed he would probably not return to Paris. 'Unless I am summoned to the Council to be tried as a heretic,' he added calmly.

'So we will not talk to you again?' Georgette cried.

Brother Thomas hesitated before replying. 'The nobleman who conceived our beliefs, Waldes, lived in Lyons, and although the Archbishop of Lyons is a dangerous opponent, there are still more members of the Poor of Christ in Lyons than elsewhere. If you should wish to learn further about our beliefs, or if you should ever decide to join our community, go to that southern city, and speak discreetly to the man who owns the baker's shop immediately to the left after you enter the town gates.'

Georgette couldn't imagine leaving the city she had grown to love. But she was moved that Brother Thomas was entrusting them with this dangerous information.

'Thank you for your offer,' she said. 'We have much to ponder on now that we have spoken with you.'

Brother Thomas bade them kneel and he put his

hands on their heads gently and blessed them. Then he departed, carrying the two French copies of the Gospels.

'Pride,' Robert said thoughtfully after the door closed. 'The self-pride that is my greatest fault. Of course, other people have thought what I think. But I assumed we were the only ones to come to such conclusions.'

Georgette was deep in her own thoughts. 'Such purity, such simple worship of Christ. There is a light and a comfort in my soul that I have not had since I was with Father David.'

Robert flushed. *Still now*, he thought, *still, even as I acknowledge my pride, I am absorbed by self. Yet Georgette is not distracted. Like a bee, she travels straight to the sweet essence.*

In the darkness before they fell asleep that night, Robert said quietly, 'I never had a true home. But when Brother Thomas was explaining, I had the strangest feeling that I saw my home ahead. I have asked our Lord to direct my steps in that path.'

Not many weeks later, Robert returned home from his classes with a heavy step. All the university was humming with reports of the Fourth Lateran Council in Rome, attended by the most powerful churchmen in Europe.

'The Council has declared the Waldensians – and several other religious sects – heretics,' he told Georgette. 'Anyone who joins them or even listens to their words will be excommunicated and may even be sentenced to death.'

Georgette gave a little gasp. Robert sat in thought, his lunch untouched. He had only one weapon against these ignorant – or willful – distortions of God's love for all men, and that was his brain. He must use it wisely, he must find a way to put it to effective and meaningful use. He did not doubt his brain, but he did doubt his courage. The Council's decree had multiplied the danger of disagreeing with the Church. Robert shivered.

CHAPTER TWENTY-FOUR

Robert was too obviously brilliant, too singleminded and unsociable, to attract friends at the university, but he did occasionally bring home for a drink of beer a few clever students for the pleasure of the philosophical arguments that followed. Georgette heard, not from her husband but from these colleagues, that Robert, despite his youth and the brief time he had studied at the university, was widely acknowledged as one of its most brilliant students.

Robert was secretly delighted by their compliments. It was a struggle for him not to boast of his successes to Georgette and he was gratified that she heard of them at these times. What he wanted most was to be accepted by the Guild of Masters as a Master of Theology so that he could teach at the university. He loved to teach and was surprisingly free of his habitual arrogance while he explained complex issues to fellow students with clarity and directness. Far sooner than he could have dreamed, an opportunity arrived.

The season for inception lectures was approaching. Final-year students who were hoping to be accepted as masters were required to deliver an inception lecture in their chosen subject before they were admitted to the Guild. They faced the daunting prospect of teaching in front of a number of esteemed masters, their fellow students, and a distinguished panel of guests.

Perhaps the most fear-inducing guests were the colourfully costumed bishops and other senior members of the clergy. The rector and the masters were frequently reminded that powerful churchmen were keeping a watchful eye on these young cloisters.

For the first time, the university had decided to offer a crowd-pleasing side show: a student from the first-year class would be selected to give a lecture too, providing a base line from which to measure the development of fully educated graduates.

Robert arrived home after his classes almost incoherent. He had been chosen as the first-year student. He was to address the collected assembly on a subject of his own choice.

Georgette flew into his arms. 'I am so proud of you, dear Robert. Praise God. If only my father were alive to be in the audience. If only the abbot . . .' He stepped out of her embrace as she faltered, but put his hands on her shoulders and looked into her face. His eyes were serious.

'Georgette, do you see how God has arranged a distance between the abbot and me so that I am not constrained by his influence on my topic? I knew the minute my name was announced that He was sending me a great opportunity. The abbot was an obstacle removed from my path. In front of a large audience, an influential audience, I have the chance to propose a more tolerant way to worship Christ.

'I began practising some phrases on my way home. Listen, Georgette: "Bloody crusades distract from the internal battles of the soul." How does that sound? And this one: "A joyous emulation of Christ's kindness rather than harsh punishment for disagreement over the minutiae of faith." What do you think?'

Georgette stared at him. He misunderstood her silence.

'Are you afraid I might sacrifice my chance to become a professor at the university, Georgette? For you know, even though I will phrase my words carefully and build my evidence tightly, it may well come to that. Or worse: I might face reprimand by the Ecclesiastical Council. The very council on which my master, the abbot, serves.' The thought of the anger of Abbot Benedict made him nauseous. 'Are you as frightened as I am?'

'Yes, I am frightened, but the reason I could not speak was because love of you overflowed my heart and deprived me of breath,' Georgette replied, taking his hands from her shoulders and kissing them. 'I know the danger as well as you. But this understanding of Christ's message found us, rather than the other way around.'

CHAPTER TWENTY-FIVE

The great hall hummed like a beehive, students busily greeting and signalling to one another, then peeling away to greet another group. It was startlingly crowded. Most graduating lectures attracted, in addition to dignitaries and venerable guests, only those students and teachers interested in the same particular area of scholarship. Sometimes a few members of the public – intellectuals too poor to attend the university, bookstore owners, writers – read the notices of lectures posted on the university gates and joined the audience. But today, for this particular lecture, there were hundreds of students from all disciplines, and a great crowd of onlookers.

The guests, honoured for their learning, money or position in the Church, were on a slightly raised dais. Even a harlequin in a street theatre could hardly have sewn such a gaudy clash of colours. Courtiers paraded in hats with dyed feathers so long and sweeping they were a danger to neighbours on all sides. The wealthy president of the Guild of Jewellers tossed his cape so that the emerald silk lining was prominently revealed and glared at the president of the Guild of Silversmiths, who had the presumption to challenge the jeweller by setting oversized rubies in his massive brooch of ornately worked silver. One diminutive churchman almost disappeared inside his ermine habit, looking unfortunately like a white rabbit without ears. Other ecclesiastical leaders corseted their portly waists in broad sashes of purple or crimson silk.

Robert stood behind the podium, pale with nervousness and looking ridiculously young. No one but he knew that Georgette had sneaked into the musicians' balcony above the great hall. From that position, she would not be revealed to the audience as the only woman in the hall, but she could give Robert encouragement, perhaps even a few guiding signals. She knew the lecture by heart, quite as well as he did.

'My colleagues, teachers, masters and lords!' Robert boomed.

Up in the balcony, Georgette winced. They had slipped into this room the previous week to practise late one night. The size of the venue had been daunting and Robert had practised throwing his voice as far as the back of the audience. But now, with adrenalin flowing,

Robert's salutation sounded too loud, as if he were shouting. Georgette lifted her arm high and made two or three quick pulses of her palm towards the ground.

Robert moderated his voice at once and she nodded her head in approval.

'I shall be talking today on a different way of drawing to Christ those souls who are not yet among His children. I must assume,' he gave a little smile, 'that it is the subject rather than my own skills that has attracted this impressive crowd.'

The students shifted and a few laughed. Georgette relaxed her shoulders a trifle. If Robert was feeling confident enough to depart from the speech and make a little joke, he would be all right.

'Of course, you are all welcome. Let us begin.'

He took a deep breath and lifted his hands, forming a large shape in the air.

'Imagine, if you will, our beloved Mother Church as a massive white statue, reaching high and glorious into the blue sky. Shining, true, magnificent. It emerges from a rocky base which is part of the earth, lined with ridges of age, marked with the dust of the ground, but solid and momentous enough to bear the weight of the shining edifice.

'Consider, gentlemen, the impossibility of separating the statue from its stone-veined roots. Imagine the danger of pounding away at the rough plinth to make the statue more pure. The battering and diminishing of the ancient rock would surely lead to cracks in the glistening white.

'Now picture the flawed and dusty base as the Jewish religion. It is accurate, for our Church rises from a Jewish base, the religion in which Jesus Christ was born and educated. And picture any cracks in the glistening white as the result of a Christian failure to behave as Christ taught us.

'For many, many years it has been the practice of the Church to obtain converts by force. The killing of heretics, the persecution of Jews, the crusades against the Muslims. Convert them or kill them. But it is clearly stated in the Gospels: we are bidden to emulate Christ by showing compassion to all people.'

Georgette scanned the audience and particularly the notable visitors on the dais. Yes, Robert's estranged benefactor, the abbot, was there, his face inscrutable. The abbot was very close to the standing council of judges. He was not liked, but it was conceded that he worked longer and harder than many of his fellow jurists. He had also taken to mortification of the flesh and it was rumoured that blood had been seen trickling from his sandals. Although he was not an old man, deep vertical lines carved his severe face.

Georgette shook her head and returned her attention to the lecture. Robert's voice was strong: articulate, reasonable, but passionate.

'. . . the Muslims. The Muslim leader who held Jerusalem against the Third Crusade was a man called Saladin, a man of scrupulous honour and justice. He, like all other Muslims, is descended from Abraham, forefather of the Jews, forefather of Jesus, and thus forefather of us all. One father on earth and, as we know for a certainty, one Father in Heaven. We are all family members. The holy book of the Muslims says . . .'

Again, Georgette's mind drifted from the familiar words, much practised in the recent evenings. There was a pressing vision in her mind – dream, memory or prophecy, she did not know – in which she was walking alongside Robert on a country road, feeling free and at peace.

Many minutes must have passed in this vivid idyll, because her attention was only drawn back to the lecture hall by a portentous quiet. Robert had reached the conclusion of his speech. He had paused and was leaning forward with great earnestness, his eyes moving intently from the face of one student to another. In the absolute quiet, his voice penetrated every corner of the hall:

'We wish to share our salvation, to bring glory to the Lord, to fulfil our religious duty, by converting the heathen. As Jesus won us with love and kindness, let us win over the Jews and the Muslims, and yes the Christians too, the Cathars and the Waldensians and others who – we say – have diverged from the Church, by showing them an example of generosity and patience, not harshness and punishment.

'May our Lord favour us all with His approval. Amen.'

The class erupted in an uproar of exclamations, but Georgette heard nothing. At the close of the lecture, Robert had raised feverishly bright eyes to her before bending his head and folding his hands in silent prayer. She followed his example.

When she opened her eyes, Georgette saw students and visitors streaming out of the hall, talking and gesturing excitedly. Her heart sank. It was customary for fellow students to rush up to the speaker and offer congratulations, but no one approached Robert. He had given an astounding show of either courage or effrontery, and it was too risky to congratulate him and perhaps be viewed as endorsing his arguments.

Georgette searched the crowd for those of Robert's fellow students who had praised him in her presence. They too were leaving, their heads lowered, without looking at the speaker. Alone on the podium, Robert looked frighteningly vulnerable. Georgette's lips trembled, but she smiled down at him, her eyes shining with love and reassurance. He gave her a strained smile in return. They would be together in a few minutes; the hall was almost empty.

There was whispering as the last few members of the audience finally departed. Georgette watched Abbot Benedict turn slowly towards the doors, hesitate with his back to Robert, and depart alone. Robert's face paled and his fingers trembled as he tidied his notes mechanically.

Georgette flew down the stone stairs and rushed into the main hall, throwing her arms around her husband.

'Robert, I am so proud,' she whispered, and a smile briefly lit his dear face.

''Tis done, Georgette. 'Tis done,' he replied. Each understood what was done.

They embraced for a long time and gradually Robert's trembling stilled and his colour returned. From the dark and intimidating hall, they walked out into the sunny afternoon.

Later, they would review every word of the lecture and worry about any possible consequences. But for now they were just two young people released from tension and suddenly ravenous with hunger.

'I have heard of an inn where they serve excellent duck à l'orange,' Robert announced. 'Not just ordinary duck but some brought specially from the country for refined palates.'

They smiled together at the memory of the fancy ducks on the cart that had brought them to Paris.

'Expensive, yes, but appropriate for this occasion, methinks. Shall we dine, esteemed wife?'

CHAPTER TWENTY-SIX

Shortly before sunrise, a knock at their door woke Georgette, who had not drunk as much sweet red wine as Robert had the previous evening. Tiptoeing to the door, she called, 'Who goes there?'

'It is I, Abbot Benedict,' came the whispered reply. 'I must speak with Robert urgently.'

Georgette was stunned. She knew Robert had been stricken by his mentor's abandonment after the lecture: the quantity of wine he had downed at the inn was an indication of more than simple relief at having the lecture behind him.

Hurrying to the bed, Georgette shook Robert hard to rouse him and then pulled a cape over her thin shift. A tall black figure slipped inside the minute Robert released the lock, and immediately closed the door behind himself.

'You are to be charged as a heretic,' the abbot began

without preamble. 'They will come to arrest you at sunrise. You must flee immediately.'

Robert had anticipated reprimand or, at unlikely worst, perhaps expulsion from the university. But he had not dreamed of arrest or trial; why, his very life was in danger. And what of the abbot? By coming to warn Robert, he had risked his entire career. Possibly his career was already damaged by his earlier connection with the student-turned-heretic.

'Thank you . . . Father,' Robert said, grasping the older man's hand in both of his own and kissing the familiar ring.

The abbot stared at him for only a moment. His anger and disappointment and fear were clear. But there was something else, a look never seen in his eyes before. It was love, a sad and lonely love. Robert's eyes glistened as he understood it all. Then Abbot Benedict slipped back out into the darkness.

It took but ten minutes to pack their few belongings into bundles not much bigger than those they had carried on the Crusade. But at that time they had not had the responsibility of Father David's precious manuscripts.

Robert hesitated, perplexed.

'You choose one that you can carry,' Georgette decided. 'And I will take another. The other five we will lock up in Father David's chest and ask the landlord to keep it safely for us.'

The landlord, stupid with sleep, was consoled for the sudden loss of his well-behaved tenants by a most generous payment for simply storing an old battered trunk. After they left, he tried the old lock, but it was solid and well made, and he could hear no clink of gold or anything precious when he shook the trunk, so he stored it in a niche under some old quilts and lost interest in his charge.

The sun was a golden half-ball on the horizon as Robert and Georgette passed through the gates of Paris, leaving behind the narrow alleyways of the city. The rains had come and the earth smelled washed and fresh. The birdsong they could barely hear inside the walls now crowded the air to bursting, and the grass was silvered with dew.

They faced towards Lyon, the same southwards direction the Children's Crusade had taken.

'Are we ready?' Robert asked.

'We are ready,' Georgette replied.

ABOUT THIS BOOK

This novel is based on historical accounts of two Children's Crusades in the summer of 1212. One was inspired and led by a twelve-year-old German boy from the town of Cologne; the other led by a twelve-year-old French shepherd called Stephen. This book is about the French Children's Crusade. With the permission of the King of France, Stephen marched thousands of youngsters, mostly between the ages of eleven and fifteen, along with a few monks and priests, all the way south to Marseilles, proclaiming that the sea would open for them and they would walk through the Mediterranean to claim the Holy Land.

The sea did not part for the pilgrims in Marseilles. Some remained in the south of France, while others attempted to return home. A large number accepted an offer of free passage to the Holy Land, sailing on seven ships operated by two men called William the Pig and

Hugh the Iron. Many years later, a priest who had seen some of those children in Egypt arrived in Marseilles with the report that the ships were captured by pirates and the children, perhaps by prior arrangement, were sent as slaves to Alexandria, Damascus and Baghdad.

Some historians put the number of participants in the Children's Crusades as high as 100,000, others as low as 5,000. No more is known than the few details above, so my story is necessarily fiction. A few historians believe that the Children's Crusades never actually happened and that the story of an army of pure young souls was Church propaganda.

It is said that the famous tale of the Pied Piper was based on the Children's Crusades, perhaps in an attempt to answer the haunting questions about why thousands chose to follow the two young leaders and why their families let them go. Better answers can be found in the religion-dominated atmosphere of that period in history.

In the thirteenth century, the western part of Europe was unified by a common Catholicism, headed by a powerful pope in Rome. The Church was teacher and unquestioned authority. Countryfolk, by far the majority of the population, were illiterate. Sons of wealthy fathers were taught by men of the Church, in Latin, but there were no schools for the poor. Peasants spoke only the local dialect and learned only the Bible stories the priests told them on Sundays, along with the tortures of Hell vividly described in church sermons. It is hard to imagine today, but there were no other sources of information or inspiration available.

The Church was also mother, father, doctor, nurse, and soup kitchen. Secular rulers of the time never considered providing their subjects with educational, medical and social welfare services. The Church was the only resource for poor and sick people, establishing hospitals run by priests or nuns and distributing food to many in dire need. Unwanted babies were left outside church doors, and travellers were welcome to stay in monasteries along the road. Work problems, marriage problems, depression and unfulfilled longings – all were laid before God, or His earthly representative, the local priest.

The Crusades began as an effort by Christians from Europe to wrest control of the land of Jesus from the Muslims who had controlled that area for almost five hundred years. The first of these Crusades, in 1099, was successful and it inspired others, which continued in waves for nearly two centuries. After the First Crusade, the others were less successful and were marked by appalling cruelty towards 'unbelievers'. The many thousands of victims included not only Muslims and Jews in the

Holy Land, but also French and Bohemian Christians who differed slightly in belief from the Church. These included the Waldensians – 'the Poor of Christ' in this book – who were labelled heretical and therefore persecuted. However, the Waldensian theme of a direct relationship with Christ, without ceremony or priestly intermediary, reemerged some centuries later in the doctrine of the new Protestant movement.

Anti-Semitism in Europe was rife at the time. Jews were restricted from almost every form of work except moneylending and trading, but those professions earned them resentment and envy, while the Church found it politically convenient to lay false blame on them for the death of Jesus. The Jews of France, England and Germany who had the misfortunate to live in defenceless, small groups along several routes taken by the Crusaders were seen as legitimate targets of brutality and looting.

In writing this book I have taken a few historical liberties. The University of Paris came to be headed by a single rector only ten to thirty years after the Children's Crusade. The Fourth Lateran Council took place in 1215. And almost two decades passed before a priest arrived in France who told the story, for the first time, of what happened to the children on seven ships supposedly bound for the Holy Land.

Recommended Books on the Crusades and Europe of that Period:

Buehr, Walter. *Crusaders*. New York: G.P. Putnam's Sons, 1959. Articulately written with imaginative descriptions.

Cosman, Madeleine Pelner. *Medieval Wordbook*. New York: Facts on File, Inc., 1996. A short and tart dictionary of words used by maids and masters, children and kings of the period.

Harpur, James. *The Crusades. An Illustrated History*. Thunder's Mouth Press, New York, 2005. Clear and well written, with numerous illustrations taken from artwork on this theme through the ages.

Ladurie, Emmanuel Le Roy. *Montaillou, The Promised Land of Error*. New York: Vintage Books, 1979. A unique insight into the everyday life of peasants in a village in southern France (Occitania) from 1318 to 1325, compiled in minute detail for the purposes of the Inquisition against the heresies of Albigensianism by a zealous and meticulous bishop-prosecutor, Jacques Fournier, who later became Pope Benedict XII.

Langley, Andrew. *Medieval Life*. Eyewitness Books series. London: Dorling Kindersley, 1996. Superb illustrations in a volume of the superb Eyewitness series.

Toussaint-Samat, M. *Stories of the Crusades*. Myths and Legends series. New York: World Pub. Co., 1966. Well-told stories and fantastical myths that grew up around the Crusades and specific noble or ignoble Crusaders.

About the author

Linda Press Wulf's first book of historical fiction, *The Night of the Burning*, won awards and inclusion in annual lists of the best fiction for young adults. She grew up in South Africa, at a time when there was no TV to distract budding readers. She lives in Berkeley, California, with her husband and two sons, and is at work on her next novel.

By the same author

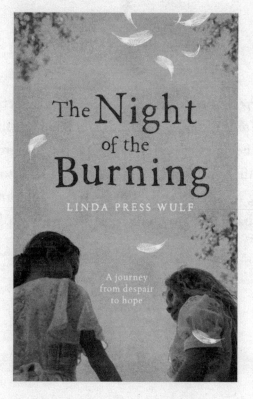

The Night
of the
Burning

LINDA PRESS WULF

A journey
from despair
to hope

'An absorbing and unforgettable read'
Financial Times

'A simply written, but extremely powerful, novel'
Robert Dunbar, *The Irish Times*

'Heartbreaking and poignant'
Kirkus Reviews